Published in the United States by Salt Heart Press.
www.saltheartpress.com

Front & back cover image by Mary Sanche.
Book design by M. Halstead.
Formatting by M. Halstead.
Interior illustrations by Leah Gharbaharan.

First printing edition 2025.

979-8-9858713-8-8

between
doorways

explorations into liminal space

edited by TJ Price

to those who said:
let's go
and then went with us

table of contents

An inbetween space bringing on dread, nostalgia, or déjà vu
whose only character is that which the observer reflects
where change waits, nothing lives, and time dies
Those places in which the ~~barrier~~ between
the self and the other is most tenuous

An unsettlingly familiar place that can both
trap and *t r a n s f o r m*

a dizzying, dangerous, hopeful blend of opportunities
between what once was, and what's yet to come

.- / .--. .-.. .- -.-. . / .-- .. - .... --- .-- -- .- -.. . / .--. .-. .-. -.-. -.-. --- ... . . ---.-.. /
.- / -. .-. .- .- -. -. -. / .... -. .- -. -.-. -. --- -. . / .-- --.-. ..-. .-. /
-. . ---. / -. .-. .-. .- .- -. . ... / .- . -. . / .-. ..-.. .- -. / -.. ... .- --.-.- /

neither here nor there; in
liminal spaces
we are only ever lost in

/ -.-.-. - .-- / .--. -.-. -.- .--. -. -. / .-. - .-. / .--.- - -- -. / -.-. --. .-. .--. /
/ ---.-- -. .-.. .- -.. -. .-. -. / .-..-.. - / .-. - .. / -- -.-. --- -. -- ..- .-.-. /

ANOMALY [dreadful]
as to create a dreadful
where THERE bleeds into HERE in such a way

once the rave has died and the drugs are wearing off
The dawnlight walk through an abandoned industrial estate

where purpose goes misplaced & memory grows forlorn
hidden places of rest, avoidance, and lack of identity
a long h a l l w a y; every door a mirror
even if you only see it from the corner of your eye
An echo of a place that somehow finds itself in corporeal form,

between two walls, the before and the after, there exists a place parallel to the now

a space to dwell forever in moments that have never come to be and never will

play space

Mob

Jess never took no for an answer. Jess was fearless. Jess knew all the best spots to hide, knew what games to play, knew what she wanted.

If Jess told you to jump off a cliff, would you?

Yeah, Mum. I trusted her more than you.

How could I trust you at all? Slumped on the sofa, TV ads plastered across your skin like melted cellophane. I was too young to know what the nodding-out meant before the kids at school never let me forget. Dad came back from business once, stood there in the dark, eyes cold, watching. Thought maybe he'd wake you up. He didn't. "Back to bed. Now." Voice monotone, just like that.

So I went. Like not-sleeping in my room was different from doing it in the hall.

Guess that's why when Jess said the doors would grant our wishes, I never questioned her. Someone had to fix everything. And it weren't gonna be you or Dad.

The final door stood in the basement of the abandoned mall off Churchside, thirteen stories down a stairwell leading nowhere. It was a slab of half-corroded metal drowned in decades of paint like rings on a tree—green and rust-red and green again, until the flaking layers slurred brown. This door wanted more than those before it, with subtle whispers that dripped into our ears.

Jess' jaw was tight. Eyes shining. She beckoned, and I hefted the rat trap.

Couldn't be sure we'd really caught a rat and not a mouse, but there was a squeak-squeak-squeak from inside the black plastic, so we must've caught something. Higher and higher it went. More and more frantic, the closer we got to the door. Like it knew what was waiting.

Maybe it did.

Looking back, that was the weirdest part. I never saw any of the doors feed. They creaked in the right places. Gave the impression of having been opened and shut in a flash of shadow and crazed hunger. But I never actually saw what happened to the rat.

Then the trap was lighter and Jess smiled in anticipation and I didn't care.

More, the door hissed.

We froze.

Jess' face fell, always quicker to anger. Not that I could blame her. "The last one only wanted an insect, what the fu—"

More.

I reached out a hand to her shoulder. She shook it off. "It's the last door," I said. "Makes sense it'd be different."

Jess slammed her fist against the wall. Bloody smear. The door quivered in anticipation. "You don't know that."

"The other doors did. Remember when it was just dreams? Just bits of paper? It's always more."

"No! You. Don't. Know."

"Don't know what?" I snapped.

"Don't know it's the last door," she said. She must've turned, cause I never forgot her expression. Desperation didn't suit her. Not when He wasn't there to force it out of her.

Strong Jess. Brave Jess.

She didn't look like that.

I was supposed to be the only one scared.

] [

Home. Chipped brickwork and broken promises. I paused on the steps, one thumb nestled in the cracks beside the front door, stained with orange brick dust, nail flicking against the moss. Neglected. Everything was. Jess' estate loomed from beyond the back garden—rows of matte-grey towerblocks biting the clouds.

Somewhere inside one of them, she crept upward towards another inevitable fight, round and round concrete stairs, spiralling nowhere.

I followed her home once. Only once.

The stairs swirled past doors which didn't speak their cost, each closed, fist-like, trapping us in the shaft. Pressure weighed on our heads. Jess' steps slowed. Story by story. Each tale warning me what to expect if He was there. How fast I should run. To hide with Mrs. Clemmons, the next floor down, who was an old dear and didn't really know what was going on but didn't like the noise, you know, the clatter of empty cans thrown from the windows, the shouting, the bangs, the dents in the walls and the just-dried spatter down by the skirting board that the child protection officers never bent to check.

We played Sonic, I think, on one of those old TVs that stuttered and growled. I couldn't focus, the blue pixel-smudge spinning through those loops like a staircase winding into the dark.

My front door swung open to an unlit hall and I tore myself away from Jess' demons. I had enough of my own.

I shucked my shoes, tracing my way by memory to the faint glow spilling from the living room where you lay wrapped in your advert-cocoon, so still I couldn't see you breathe. I shut the room closed with a click and stood there in the dark, not seeing you at all.

It felt better. Just slightly.

A ready meal waited—not in the microwave—but near enough it suggested an attempt at effort. I loaded the rest of the shopping delivery into the fridge and made dinner.

You wouldn't check I'd eaten. You wouldn't check the missed messages from the school board asking where I was. You wouldn't ask me how my day had been and I'd never tell you how scared I was—scared about the cat or dog I'd need to find to feed that door in the basement of the mall; scared of letting Jess down; scared what she might be facing right now, in a house worse than my own. Scared one day I'd come back and you'd've died in those wrappings of flickering colour or hatched and flown away and left me nothing at all.

I hated you, I think. Not like brave Jess did with fire and rage, but a quiet thing, slinking unacknowledged in the back of my mind when I couldn't drown it with yearning for better times.

I wanted my old mum back, the mum of my fading memories. I'd feed doors with almost anything they asked for, if they could just wake you up and force you to be a parent again.

I never could imagine being able to change you alone.

Yeah, it must've been my hate for you that kept me frozen in that kitchen with a fork clutched in my fist and shitty shepherd's pie cooling in front of me. Cause I couldn't quite bring myself to catch one of the neighbourhood cats and drag it—yowling and clawing—to a basement that shouldn't exist in Churchside.

It must've been my hate for you, Mum. I'd hate to think I was just so terribly scared that a cat might not be enough. I couldn't have been that much of a coward.

Not to my only friend.

] [

I didn't find a cat.

The road to the mall passed with a tight chest and strained breaths—one for each pace, a constant tension borne by the lack of carrier by my side. A ginger tom watched me pass from the upper window of the corner shop one block from the mall, fat and smug. I didn't walk to the front doors; instead, I slipped round back and through the chain-link we'd cut all those months before, unsnagging my already-torn hoodie from the crooked wires.

Jess stood at the staff entrance, weight shifting from one foot to the other. That door had been open the whole time. Never did find out whether it had a cost, if the builders just forgot to close it when they ripped the shop units clear, or if the building just opened itself some quiet night, ready to invite us in.

"Where's the cat?" Jess said.

She'd stolen makeup again. Inexpertly applied. Insufficient to cover the dull-purple bruise on her right cheek.

I shrank in my hood. "I couldn't find one."

She flinched.

That was worse, I think, than shouting straight away.

"Really?" Her voice was a whisper.

"Really."

She didn't move. Frozen. Just her breath speeding up, gradually, until her shoulders heaved like bad stop-motion.

"I'm sorry," I said.

My eyes were hot, cheeks cold. Guess that's why I didn't see the woman until she was right pressed up against the fence, glaring at us.

Jess did, though, and she glared right back.

"What're youse doing in there? Trespassing?" The woman spoke in quick, clipped tones, like she couldn't imagine anyone interrupting her. "It's unsafe. Get out this instant."

My mind raced. Excuses, distractions, anything to put off that dangerous tension in Jess' hunched frame.

"Playing," my mouth said, before my brain caught up.

"Playing?" the woman repeated, as though it was a slur. *"Playing?"*

"Not like there's many playgrounds, and the adults don't want us round the estate and the older kids don't want us near the pub, so yeah, playing, I guess?"

All she had to do was nod. Nod and mutter in that way adults did about disappointments and the state of things and unknown pasts when things were better.

She didn't.

The woman drew herself up, a lacquered green nail picking at the fence, gaze searching for how we'd gotten in. "It's school hours."

She should've stopped there. She really should've stopped there.

"Where's your parents?" the woman said.

I closed my eyes.

"Mind your own, you fucking hag. It's safer." I heard Jess say.

I only caught the employee door bouncing back open off its useless lock, the snatch of Jess' dirty-blonde hair; the faint, wet scent of the depths, sweet with decay.

Then the woman was screaming obscenities, and panic filled my mind with noise. I left her there at the fence, caught up in her outrage but with enough mind to spot our entrance and squeeze herself through after us, one cardigan button tugged free and clattering to the ground.

I ran after Jess.

I knew where she'd gone, even without her trainers slap-slapping back to me off slanted walls bow-backed with damp. Each cracked floor-tile clawed for my heels, the pools of shadow between the shop units deeper and darker than they ever had been before. I could lose myself in them. Drown. Be dragged downwards before I reached the service tunnel and that strange interrupted wall where the first door stood open and waiting.

It had only wanted dreams, scrawled on paper and slipped through its hinges. How far we'd come. How very far.

Blonde flicked. Vanished.

I hesitated.

Sweat-slicked hair clung to me, tickling my eyelids. You used to sweep it clear, once, Mum. Tell me I was clever. Tell me I was brave. Maybe if you'd believed it, I would have too. Maybe I wouldn't have even looked at that hungry door, its gap-toothed smile peeking from the wall panels.

The stairs spiralled into the dark. Down thirteen floors that shouldn't have been there at all. Going nowhere. No escape.

The woman's heels echoed through the mall's carcass, discordant, overlapped with shouted threats—legal action and safety and anger, anger, anger.

She'd find us soon. Track the footprints in the dust. Smell us above the grime and that pervasive, moist reek of below. It's your fault I ran on. Your fault I ignored the doors' whispers and hid in the battered supply closet at the corridor's end, where long-separated paint dripped a permanent stain.

You drowned your fears, Mum. I drowned *in* them.

That click-click-click of heels passed me by, barely paused in panting disbelief of the door and its strange staircase, and slipped from hearing—slowly muffled, then gone.

I don't know how long I waited, shivering. Long enough for the thin metal to fog completely. Long enough I started wondering why the woman hadn't stampeded back up, with Jess kicking and screaming and fighting back in that way she'd had to her whole life.

Metal creaked. I spilled from the closet. Down the hall, the first door stayed put, sneering at my panic.

I had to know. I needed to see. I wanted Jess to be safe, to not have done anything stupid. I really did. But I think deep down, I knew.

I don't remember the descent.

Jess met me with a broken-mirror smile.

Blood flowed from scratches on her arm, tinted to off-brown murk by the green nail lacquer at their edge. Behind her, more of it pooled on the floor, huge and dim and still spilling from beneath the woman's hairline as she lay slumped there, just-about-alive.

Each rise and fall came weaker than the last, jerky in the half-light. Bordered by concrete and moss and that vivid red pool.

"Jess . . ." I said.

"She fell."

I stared at the smeared makeup above the bruise on Jess' cheek and the blood on her arm and the blood on the floor and the wall and the woman dying.

"She fell," Jess said, the phrase tailing into soft, jagged laughter. "She fell, yeah? Tell me she fell."

"She fell," I whispered. I wanted it to be true.

We stood by the thirteenth and final door and watched that huge pool of blood shrink as it vanished beneath the sill. Watched the woman's rises rise less and her falls fall further.

More, the door hissed.

Jess shook, just once. Her face screwed tight. I recognised her hate, and the yearning that came with it.

More.

"Help me move her? Please?" she said.

] [

I don't have dreams anymore. I don't wish for a parent who never returned, who choked in their own vomit and left me so terribly alone. I just have nightmares.

It's your fault, Mum.

If I hadn't hated you, I could've just killed a fucking cat.

I could've spoken to Jess again.

I could've brought you back.

I wouldn't have to live in fear of halls and famished doors and staircases winding into the dark. Of the pieces of Him they found leaking through the floor that gave poor Mrs. Clemmons a heart attack. Of where Jess might've gone, and what she might still be doing, after she vanished.

Please understand, Mum.

I needed to hate you. It was the inevitable end of your spiral—overdosing in that shitty house, surrounded by rotting food you never put away by yourself, waiting for a man who never cared enough to wake you up.

I realise you needed that.

Or my life would've been so much worse, knowing what had been sacrificed to make things right. I needed you to die.

For everything to end.

So leave me in peace, Mum. It's the least you could do.

Fun-a-Lot

DEMI-LOUISE BLACKBURN

The last summer me and Jenny ever spent together was a washout. Slow, heavy, and sticky. Oncoming college was a bit of grit stuck in the corner of our eye, irritating and ever-present.

I wasn't sleeping well. I'd stir, half-dreaming, convinced a wad of straw was lodged in my throat. I couldn't swallow it, couldn't throw it up. I'd reach into my mouth and pull, but the strands were slippery and endless. I had to just lay there. Suffocating and itching from the inside.

My Mam said it was nerves over moving up a year. She'd had the same problem when work stressed her out—only in *her* dreams, her teeth would crumble to shards and she'd swallow the pieces, fillings and all.

I moped through town most evenings, Jenny in tow, both of us dodging nagging parents, our pockets light, and no pub willing to overlook our age. The riverbank was too clotted to venture down, with rotten pink flowers that stunk of cat piss. They'd padlocked the scrapyard after kids a town over set it ablaze two years back. So we'd haunt the fortnightly car boot sale at the old flour mill, rummaging through childhood memories marked three for a pound, then wander back home.

My house was a no-go. Dad worked nights in a warehouse and, during the day, he woke at the drop of a pin. At my begging, we holed up in Jenny's attic bedroom. Her Mam worked long hours in the town centre, and her stepdad spent his time watching films in the living room, off his face with pain meds for a bad back. He'd always been alright with us. Never really cared what we did, how loud we were, so long as we stayed out of his way.

That, too, soured in the heat.

The last time I visited, he was smoking in the living room, eyes glazed and roaming us. The atmosphere seemed off even before I dialled into the noises coming from the television. A lick of panic dripped down my spine when I heard it—panting and groaning.

I didn't see what was playing. But I knew.

Another pocket of our summer holidays turned to rot, and all Jenny's stepdad did was smile, the hand on his crotch twitching, asking for us to come watch.

We'd run up those stairs like ghosts were nipping at our heels. Vacancy erased Jenny's face for the rest of the night. I laughed, but it was slow and forced, when I dared to comment on how weird it was, how he must not have even noticed what was playing, how he must be so embarrassed.

Jenny's gentle voice admitted, not long after, "He's been doing this a lot, lately."

I woke that night, fighting the covers off my sweaty legs, my hands on my chest, feeling for hay in my lungs. When, at last, I calmed and turned to my side, I caught Jenny staring at me. She didn't speak. Just looked through the dark, through me, tears streaming down her face.

I couldn't ask. Didn't dare.

And I don't think Jenny could've told me what was happening, even if she wanted to.

] [

The next morning, we wandered old haunts. It was easier to look backwards, for Jenny at least. High school ending was enough to calcify her into a girl-shaped shell for weeks after Leavers' Day. She'd applied for the same classes at the same college as I, praying we'd stay glued together, but I hoped we wouldn't be. Not every class, not every day. It grated on me, now and again, like feeling warm wet breath on the back of your neck all the time.

Our first port of call was Moore Primary, where we'd met as kids. Off season, the building looked cold and deflated. The playground was full of litter, blown in between the railings that hemmed the area off from the surrounding roads. We headed around the side of the school, trying the gates, hoping they might budge, but everything was locked tight.

Defeated, we perched at a bus stop out on the main road, watching one, two, three buses pass by, and grimaced at the passengers. I was about to ask Jenny if she remembered the dumping ground our parents sent us to for most of our summers, when she said: "Fun-A-Lot. That's around here somewhere, right?"

I studied her profile as I spoke. "That's well weird."

"What?"

"I was literally just thinking about it. We used to have our birthday parties there all the time, didn't we?"

"Never mind birthday parties," Jenny said, gaze moving from her shoes to the road, where two men were shouting at each other through their car windows. "It was like every summer holiday until the park down Botley Road got built up. Surprised we didn't get scurvy or whatever, we were pale as milk."

"Scurvy? That's when you don't eat fruit, dickhead."

Jenny laughed, her smile wide and gummy and lovely. "Shut up. You get what I mean."

We sat a while longer in comfortable silence, but Fun-A-Lot was stuck in my head, like food between my teeth. A blur of whitewashed bricks and wobbly climbing frames; yellow foam; sluggish kiddie rides. A long, beige corridor with a door at the end, shut tight until special occasions.

"Shall we have a mooch round, see if it's still there?" I asked, but Jenny was already on her feet.

] [

It wasn't too hard to find. The primary school was the gap-toothed face to a set of narrow, winding roads which used to be the town's high street, only now most of the shops were gone, empty or converted into flats. Everywhere we looked seemed pockmarked with vacancy.

We doubled back on ourselves a few times, lost in alleyways or in back gardens, midday heat beating at our backs, until we heard the screech of a saw and metal tools being chucked aside. In a flood, I remembered the play centre was on the same stretch of road as an old backstreets mechanic, and we followed the noise.

A large plywood board came into view, smothering three or four house lengths, with a childish mural of animals painted on it. A sun-bleached vulture squawked out a list of opening times, followed by a trio of big cats with their arms around each other. At the end, a snake curled around a picket-fence sign, directing drivers around the corner for the car park.

FUN-A-LOT, it read, squashed above it all in red and blue graffiti.

"God, it's rougher than I remember." Jenny said.

"It was always a bit of a shithole, to be fair." I agreed.

"Don't mince your words."

"A *proper* shithole."

Jenny rolled her eyes and crossed the road, leaving me to trail behind her. "How much you betting it's still open?" she asked.

"No chance," I said. "Doesn't exactly look like it's been freshened up lately, does it?"

We followed the faux-picket sign to where grinding metal roared, and a large glass pane down the side of Fun-A-Lot allowed us a glance into the play centre.

Deep into the bowels of the room, a four-story climbing frame occupied the shadow, pressed against the walls, floor to ceiling. Its limbs were protected by blue and yellow foam, the open frames on the higher floors blocked off with red mesh. On the left, a slide went from top to bottom, leading into a ball pit.

"Déjà vu," Jenny said, her voice a little off.

Past the window, another picket marked an open gate into the car park, and we followed until the entrance greeted us. The overhang of the roof cast the doorway in thick shadow, as though someone had taken a small slice of the building clean off and left nothing in its place. Cut off your nose to spite your face, I idly thought.

Unease started to clamp down at the back of my neck, like I was a cat being picked up by its scruff. I looked to the guttering, expecting to see a camera, or an alarm, imagining the owner watching us, waiting for us to break in —but there was nothing.

It lacked the air of an abandoned building. Felt different, somehow, from the surrounding roads and their dying township. Perhaps it was because Fun-A-Lot had always felt a little rundown, a little broken, even as children. Perhaps it was the way pockets of roof tiles slumped down like heavy eyelids. At any moment, I expected the building's wooden frame to snap to attention, for an essence of it to wake.

Jenny cupped her hands over the glass of the door and looked inside.

"We'll look like right freaks if anyone catches us here," I warned. "Watch it still be up and running."

Jenny pulled away and shook her head. "Definitely isn't. The till on reception's gone." With that, she pushed hard on the door. Nothing. She pushed again, and again, and when it finally caved, an anvil dropped into my stomach. The wood caught on the floor and screamed, as though too big for the frame.

"Jen, what the fuck are you doing?"

She peeked around the corner of the door. "What's it look like?"

Then, I lost Jenny to the gloom of Fun-A-Lot.

I didn't want to go inside. I expected nostalgia to pique my curiosity, a fondness to return, but it never quite arrived. I looked through the doorway's glass, into the murk, and I felt deceived. Lied to. As though someone had rebuilt my Fun-A-Lot, detail by detail, expecting no one to ever know. A childhood teddy replaced by a brand new doppelgänger.

"Jenny? Come on, I'm not spending all day inside this dump," I called out. No reply came, and so I followed. The door promptly shut behind me, as though coiled tight as a spring.

Inside, I was greeted by a counter, the alcove behind it leading into the kitchens. The walls were littered with a mixture of badly-painted animals, distorted and dimpled by the texture of bricks behind, and there were a slew of advertisements for local shops and services tape-stuck on top. Laundrettes, car repairs, mobile hair stylists.

We'd trespassed before, in beaten-up old houses and shops, but they at least held reminders of their occupants, proof we weren't the first to let curiosity push us inside for a moment or two before leaving. Graffiti, tab ends, condoms, beer cans, carrier bags, rat droppings, dead birds— disgusting and distasteful, but signs of life. There was none of that here.

The right side of the building opened out into the heart of the play area, where the climbing frame watched over the room. Jenny stood in the centre of the open space, dim light from the window behind licking up her back. Even surrounded by highchairs and walkers, her shadowed form appeared small. She craned her head up towards the ceiling, peering into the dark upper platforms of the climbing frame, sparing me a glance as I walked further inside.

"I thought it'd look tiny, now we've grown a bit," she said. "But it still looks massive."

She was right. It seemed to go on for miles—the precious bit of sunlight drifting in from the windows hardly touched the edges of its form.

"Yeah, it does," I admitted. "Looks creepy as hell."

"Creepy?" Jenny's face crumpled. "Don't you think it's kind of sweet?"

"Sweet?"

"Yeah, like . . . I dunno. When you have a clear-out at home, and find old toys and stuff? Just feels good to remember. Right cute."

I hummed, brushed down a tabletop, surprised at the lack of dust, and sat down. "I guess."

"I kinda miss being that little, lately." And there was the voice again.

(He's been doing this a lot, lately)

"Things'll get better at college," I lied. "We'll have a bit of freedom for once."

Jenny's shoulders tensed, dropped, and I had the awful sensation that I'd said something wrong. She offered me a thin smile. The muddy light slinking into the room caught on every dip of her face. She looked old. Weathered. "Yeah . . . yeah, maybe." She sighed. "Wanna try the slide with me?"

I shook my head. "Get fucked. I can feel the spiders crawling on me from here."

"God, when did you get to be such a wimp?"

Jenny clambered through an archway and into the climbing frame, smacking her head on the first platform twice before she hunched over. It looked like she was squatting inside a puckered red mouth. A wave of disquiet flooded me, but Jenny didn't seem to notice. She looked elated.

"Grow up, it's probably disgusting in there," I said.

"It's not that bad," Jenny replied, voice muffled, crawling up a set of foam logs, laughing to herself when she slipped once or twice. Even from where I sat, I saw the exhaustion falling off her, shedding like old skin. She really did look like a child.

Irritation started to get the better of me. I didn't want to be there. At all. I loved Jenny, more than I'd ever let on, but watching her scramble about inside that kid's play area made me feel unmoored. A rush of heat rose to my face, and I ground my teeth. For a moment, they felt alarmingly pliant.

I got up from the table, prodding and checking each tooth with my tongue, and didn't turn when Jenny got inside the tube on the top platform, whooping as she slid down into the ball pit.

I'd all intentions of leaving, waiting outside, until she noticed I'd gone. But then I saw the sign for the party room—cherry-red, at the end of a pale corridor.

I never understood why they kept it closed aside from birthdays. Fun-A-Lot always had a tacky air to it. Weather-worn and tired, it was the childhood equivalent to booking out a working men's club for a family gathering. Not offensive. Just cheap and cheerful. But the party room, compared to the rest of Fun-A-Lot, was truly depressing.

It was a small, white-washed room with no windows, wooden rafters set into a ceiling so dark it looked like the ribbed, wet flesh of a yawning mouth. Little light seeped in from the open door, but it was enough to see what felt like a hundred sets of tables and chairs—tiny, toddler-sized place-holders. Only one wall was decorated with a mural: a faded, spindly giraffe whose head disappeared into the murk of the roof. Around it, children's drawings, in paint and cheap oil pastels.

Despite the gnawing in the back of my mind, I softened a little at the pictures and moved closer, squinting against the dark. Most were a blur of colours and shapes, names neatly written in marker by a parent or worker. Some I even recognised as classmates we'd long since grown apart from.

And, at the top, where the shadow bled down into the room, a drawing of two girls in red and blue paint, smiling.

Signed by *Jenny, age five.*

Behind me, the door eased shut.

I heard it as it clicked into the frame, followed by the even pace of footsteps retreating down the hall. It was Jenny, of course. Could only be Jenny. But my heart kicked once, twice, then ran away from me. Above, the metal of a vent groaned. I weaved between the chairs, arms out to steady myself, when I caught my shins on a table, and pulled the party room door open.

The hallway was awash in yellow light. Fluorescents hummed. To my right, a muffled child's voice erupted, and I screamed in reply.

Thank you! Press the orange button to add another coin, or press the start button to go! Hold on tight!

A washing machine rumble followed. A kiddie ride, hidden in shadow at the dead end of the corridor, burst into light, the lime-green tractor rocking back and forth, a tinny banjo playing over the speaker.

"Shit," I whispered, and the lead in my shoes eased. I rushed to the opening of the corridor, calling out for Jenny, furious we'd been caught.

I looked inside the climbing frame, dreading the inevitable shouting when the owner caught us. Yet I was struck with the same, uneasy feeling as before—that something just wasn't quite right. I tried to put my finger on it.

The closest thought that came was a vague shape of a memory. Eyes squeezed shut, and a molar-shaped indent in my inner cheek, stifling a laugh as my Dad opened the bedroom door, checking I was in bed while I pretended to sleep. He'd always known I was pretending. You can tell when someone isn't quite there.

Above, the party bunting swayed, and a hidden radio played decades-old pop tracks, low and rasping. A horrible smell came with the cold air: ocean spray, and stale urine. I glanced towards the front desk, and in the kitchen behind it, I heard cutlery rattling.

Thump.

On the top platform of the climbing frame, the uppermost segment of the slide shuddered. A dark shape sat within the tube, like the shadow of a fish below the surface.

"Jenny? Jenny, come on, we've gotta go," I begged.

All around me, the air felt suspended. The climbing frame remained absent of swarming children. The owner was nowhere to be seen. The only response came in the form of another thud, a hand slapping the plastic of the slide, then fists, pounding. I called out again, anger flooding me, until I wondered if Jenny was actually stuck.

"For fuck's sake," I hissed, casting another nervous glance around before running to the mouth of the climbing frame. The floor was freezing beneath my knees as I shuffled up the foam logs, hunched over, pushing hair from my eyes, moving up the platforms until I found the entrance to the slide.

At first, I didn't see a thing, just the empty, endless guts of the red slide. The pounding fists stopped. I was left alone, for a moment, with the kiddie ride's disembodied narrator, eerily distant, my ears prickling at every small sound. The crack of plastic unsticking from my legs, the vents above groaning as they cooled, and then, from the slide, deep and laboured breathing.

It was a prank. I knew it was. Had to be. Jenny suspended against a curve in the tube, waiting to make me jump. But why wasn't she lurching out of the tunnel with a scream already? My shirt stuck to my skin, sweat pooling at the back of my neck.

Caught in a stalemate, I crawled forward, dipping my head inside the warm, humid entrance. My head snagged, again, on the image of a mouth, a throat, as if Fun-A-Lot were just a series of enormous, looping windpipes. The baby hairs on the top of my head caught on a breeze, a breath. My pulse pounded in my wrists, the bend of my arm. Teeth clacked together in my head.

Further in, tipping forward, I discovered mousey-blonde hair, tangled and damp. A hand gripped the curve of the plastic, holding on. Inside, the pungent, ammoniac smell swelled. Jenny's fingers were pale and wrinkled, as if she'd been washing them for hours. Suddenly, I was terrified to reach out for her. What if I gripped onto her hand, and her skin slipped away, like a glove?

"Jenny? Jen? Hey, are you alright?"

I shuffled further in, bile in my throat. The hand twitched. Extended. Pulled. Jenny raised her head to see me.

I caught wet, bloodshot eyes. The deep, sweet scent of knitting wounds. Bruised, pulsing veins at Jenny's temples, beneath her eyes—and then she dropped.

The noise that ricocheted through the slide could've been laughter, could've been screaming. I pulled my body out of the slide in time to see Jenny running between tables and chairs, down toward the party room, swaying as though drunk. The lights flickered.

For a long time, I sat back on my knees, my view of Fun-A-Lot distorted by red mesh, and didn't dare move. My bladder felt full. Sweat pearled against my clammy skin. I was too afraid to call out. What if I shouted, screamed, and nothing at all came back? Not the owner, not Jenny, not even a ghost of my own voice. More than being caught, I was terrified of finding myself alone. Defenceless.

Inch by inch, I scrambled out of the climbing frame, the sight of the slide too suffocating to contend with, knocking my head as I rushed down the squat platforms. I gave the corridor a passing glance as I emerged, found it slumbering, aside from the gentle rocking of the kiddie ride, and a shudder ran through me.

At the entrance, I was struck again by the vacancy of the front desk, and I took the chance to try the door. It was the same as when we'd arrived. Shut tight, like it hadn't even been built with neither entry nor exit in mind. I didn't have the strength to force it open, even with my entire weight balanced against it. I needed Jenny. I needed help, but . . .

Thank you! Press the orange button to add another coin, or press the start button to go! Hold on tight!

I retraced my steps. Once more I stood at the mouth of that long, beige corridor, the crimson walls of the party room winking out at me. The kiddie ride hushed as I approached. Silence gripped the building. My breaths came ragged and tight.

Minutes stretched by until I plucked up the courage to stand before the cherry-red door of the party room. As I pressed my hand against the cold wood, the gnawing panic in my head turned to frightened, feral gnashing. I listened out. Low murmurs escaped from beneath the bottom of the door.

(he's doing this all the time)

(nothings the same)

(i'm always so tired)

(i know, i know, i know)

(there's nothing for me)

(she's listening)

I opened the door.

Jenny's mouth clamped shut so quickly I heard teeth crack. She was faced away from me, at the mural, pressed against the sea of children's paintings, shadow bleeding down atop her. I didn't dare look up. I kept my eyes pinned on the back of Jenny's head. All the while, the ceiling breathed, and somehow, I knew—it was tasting the air.

My voice came, whispered and wet. "Jenny?"

She groaned, hiccuped, like a child reluctantly waking.

"Jenny, we have to go." I said.

She shook her head, paper rustling, the shadow licking at tendrils of her hair. "It's so sweet here," she said.

(So sweet.)

"Jenny, please. Come help me with the door. Let's go."

"I don't want to."

She turned to face me.

A sharp, animalistic fear responded, and drove me to slam the door shut. My tongue was laced with the taste of blood and dirt and pus. I backed away, leaning a shoulder on the wall for support, one hand clamped over my mouth, thoughts pounding around my skull. With each step back, I heard its twin.

The door opened.

Three pale, fused fingers curled over the frame. Bulging, swollen grey eyes followed, their lids glued shut and paper-thin, the dark swell of them visible through a window of stretched red skin, the eyeballs behind rolling as though dreaming. Jenny emerged, into the light of the hallway. A frail, crooked body hunched, stumbling after me.

As she pursued, the building shuddered. Its walls expanded, retracted, expanded, like lungs. It breathed. Inhaled. Stole from her. The lights hissed, then burned brighter. Another breath and the fixtures popped in warning. Jenny's form cracked in response. Her form tightened. Thinner flesh, finer hair, until she was made of translucent pink velvet. A baby mouse. Reducing with each step towards me.

Another breath, and the kiddie ride's speaker exploded into high-speed banjo plucks, overcharged and rabid. It jostled, back and forth, until its momentum nipped at Jenny's meagre shadow, the electric cord taut like a dog on a chain. By the time we reached the mouth of the hallway, Jenny was a nautilus curl of spider-veins and bloated, white-blue innards.

In the main room, the speakers crackled and wailed with children sobbing. One chair scraped on the floor, followed by another, each flying back from the tables as phantom infants left their seats and rocketed around the room, around my knees, their ghosts tugging at my legs, pulling me towards the shambling horror before me, begging me to stay.

"Jenny," I gasped, resisting, stumbling backwards over charity shop toys, tripping over three-for-a-pound dolls and teddies and plastic zoo animals, falling onto second-hand memories. My head clipped the floor as I dropped. Spots erupted in my vision. Warmth flooded my jeans.

My lungs were on fire like hay fields burning. Teeth turning to rot. All of me falling apart.

I kicked backwards, shuffling away, pain ringing in my ears, until my back hit the door. I scrambled to my feet and risked turning from her, pulling at the door with everything I had left, my shoulder cracking as I heaved my weight backwards. The sweat on my palms slipped against the handle and I stumbled. Hot, sour breath pressed down on the back of my neck. Close. She was close. Wet and warm and nibbling.

Jenny sighed through a throat swollen and pregnant— whatever was lodged deep inside her, soaking her in—and said: "Stay with me?"

(Stay with me?)

"I can't," I said, and she inhaled the words, long and slow, a piece of me breaking off.

But that wasn't right. I could stay with her. Forever, if I wanted.

"I don't want to!" I screamed, and with it, my chest finally cleared, the pain swallowed up or spat out or burned away to nothing but a burst of ash.

With a deep gasp, I pulled again, and the door cried as it opened. I forced myself through the gap, wood clawing at my bare arms, and stumbled out of Fun-A-Lot's mouth, away from Jenny's begging sobs, and out onto the warmth of sun-baked gravel.

] [

The sun was dropping fast by the time I opened my eyes again. Starlings cut through the evening sky, their calls weak against the beat of a thousand small, black wings. I hadn't slept. Hadn't passed out. Just laid on the ground with my eyes tight shut, existing. It felt as though I'd been away from the world for decades.

Behind me, a Jenny-shaped shell gasped and wheezed and cried on the threshold, curled in on itself, expelling things neither of us could name, letting go of all its secrets. Letting go of everything, and Fun-a-Lot slurped up her spill.

In time, I imagined there'd be nothing left of my friend at all. A wet shadow of her body against the floor—half-in, half-out of Fun-A-Lot's jaws. And then that, too, would evaporate in the sticky summer heat.

Part of me felt I should look back. Acknowledge her. Imprint Jenny in my mind, even like this. But I couldn't bear to look at her—at it—again.

I closed my eyes a moment longer, found a pale, waxen halfling imprinted against my eyelids. Spider-veins and the soft, pale underbellies of snakes. A baby bird spilled from its shell. A creature deep from the ocean brought upside, collapsing under its own, terrible weight.

And, deeper, beyond the dark of my closed eyes, a smile: wide and gummy and lovely. A smile nothing could devour.

the death factory

CARSON WINTER

It all started when Gaspar came running up to us on the
playground. We were twelve—too old for the swing set—
but that's where we were. Joe and I were just learning to
practice irony, to embrace shame. But Gaspar, somehow,
hadn't figured it out yet—he still acted like a kid. It was his
exuberance, I think. While we sat on the swing set, affecting
coolness, Gaspar would throw himself recklessly into the
seat and swing. He'd try to wrap the chains around the bar.
He'd jump out and proudly mark his landing in the sand and
then run back to the swing and try again. He was always
acting like a kid. So, when Gaspar came running to us, Joe
and I had already iced over in retaliation.

"I saw something," he said.

"Cool," said Joe.

"No, really," said Gaspar. "Our parents. They were at the factory."

"Whose parents?"

"Our parents. Your parents, my parents. Everyone's parents."

Joe cocked an eyebrow. "My parents were home last night."

"Not at midnight."

"Mine were out at dinner," I said, unsure if I had heard them come home. "Did you see them?"

"Yes!" said Gaspar. "There were there."

"At the factory?" I asked.

He nodded. Every kid in town had played at the factory at one point or another. An enormous cube with broken windows, deep in the heart of our industrial center. All three of us had breathed its dusty air, climbed its glaciers of plaster and particle board, thrown rocks at its derelict machines just to hear the echoing clank.

"What were they doing?"

"Praying."

Joe asked, "How do you know?"

"Because I was there. I followed them."

"Praying?" I asked.

Gaspar nodded, in that excited way little kids do, and I almost felt like I was going to hit him. "Yep. I saw them. They all walked there around midnight, then climbed to the third floor and got down on their knees."

"That doesn't mean they were praying," I said. "You don't know what they were doing."

"No," he said. "But don't you want to know?"

We were at the age then that the idea of our parents having a life separate from us seemed unbelievable. They lived with us, they fed us, they asked us how our days went, but they did not exist without us. Or at least, I couldn't imagine them existing without us.

I wanted to push the thought of my parents going to the factory aside because it did not seem to be the type of thing a parent would do. Going to the factory was what kids did. The idea of them traipsing to the same rotting building made me sick to my stomach.

Joe and I exchanged cautious glances, obviously intrigued, but unwilling to validate Gaspar's story with active interest.

That day we told him we didn't care. And then after, I went home and thought of nothing but the factory.

] [

Throughout the week, our interest grew alongside Gaspar's story. The prayers were now accompanied by a loud, mechanical hum that shook the whole factory.

"Like an engine," he said, with wild eyes. "Like a lawnmower or something, but huge."

"We'll need to wait till next week," said Joe. "Because they probably go only one time a week. If they're praying, that is."

"Like church," I said.

"Right, exactly. Like church. So, that means they go at the same time every week. On Mondays, right, Gasp?"

"Yeah, that's right. Late Monday nights."

] [

Sitting at the dinner table, I tried to question my parents, who sat very normally, as if nothing was wrong at all.

"Mom," I said. "Are we religious?"

She thought for a moment. "No, not really. Would you like us to be?"

Dad looked up. "Is someone at your school religious, is that what this is?"

"Well, no—"

"Don't need anyone filling your head with that nonsense."

Mom cast him a withering glance. "It's okay if he has religious friends. There's nothing wrong with going to church. For some people, it can fill a void and be a very welcome addition to one's life."

"But not for us, right?"

"We weren't really raised with it," she said. "It just wasn't a good fit, I guess. But, if you want to learn about different religions, surely we could arrange something. A class, perhaps?"

I moved peas around my plate in a circle. "No, no, that's okay. I was just wondering if we had a religion. That's all. If we ever, you know, pray?"

The room was very quiet. The only sound was the squeaking of peas on my plate. I dared not look up. I realized I was holding my breath.

Finally, Dad said, perhaps too naturally, "Prayer? Is that what they're teaching him at school?"

Mom shook her head. "There's nothing wrong with asking questions." Then, she turned to me, her eyes bright and sharp like a polished blade. "No, honey, we don't pray."

I felt then suddenly, as if there was a great elaboration waiting on her tongue—a revealing *but, honey,* and I was left watching those sharp eyes, anticipating silence.

Dinner continued with idle small talk—a sense of forced normalcy that made me unbearably anxious. My legs were shaking under the dinner table, electric with nervous energy.

When I got up to go to my room, knees wobbling, my father grabbed me by the arm as I passed. "No more thinking about how things fit together. Right, son?"

His touch was firm, almost painful. "Yes, sir."

He let me go and I ran straight to my room.

The next day, Joe and Gaspar had similar stories.

"They were acting weird, right?" Gaspar seemed validated by this fact, much to my chagrin.

"Yes," I admitted. "At least, I thought so."

"Knew it."

"My Dad said we were Catholics," said Joe. "But then he said there was more out there than we'll ever know."

"That's not that weird," I said. "Maybe he's just being, like, open-minded."

But Joe, in rare form, brooded. "No. It wasn't like that at all. It was weird. It was like he was trying to tell me something without telling me it." He paused. "I was scared of him."

We all sat quiet, even Gaspar, our feet dragging on the earth beneath the swing set as we hung, suspended, waiting for an answer.

"Is it a cult?" I asked.

"It's a group," said Joe matter of factly. "Can a group become a cult?"

Gaspar shrugged. "Sure. Why not?"

We were playing a game of boyish semantics. I offered, "A congregation?"

"Yes, maybe. That can be a church, or something like it. A place where people gather to worship," said Gaspar.

Joe, suddenly angry, said, "But were they worshiping or praying?"

"Is there a difference?"

"Yes," he said, his teeth clenched. "There's a difference."

"I don't know then. Maybe both."

We considered that for a moment.

Joe sighed. Then, his head lifted. "What if it's a fellowship?"

"A fellowship?"

"It could be," said Gaspar. "We don't know what it is. It could be anything."

"Why a fellowship?" I asked.

Joe's hands were white on the chains. "I just think it fits. Like, it's a club, maybe. Or people, like, joined together under a common cause. A purpose. That's sort of what a fellowship is, right?"

"Yeah, I guess," I said. I was already trying to think: what club could my parents possibly belong to?

The bell rang. Over the last couple days, we'd begun to consider the fact that all of our teachers might be in this fellowship too. The idea of being locked up in a classroom with them filled me with cool dread.

"We need to go inside," said Gaspar.

The second bell rang.

I sighed. My throat tightened. "I don't know why we're acting like this. It was just a story Gaspar told. He probably made it up. Nothing's wrong, right?"

I expected Joe to come with me on this journey of reassurance, but he shook his head no. "Sorry, dude. You didn't see my dad."

And Gaspar just sat there and I think I could tell for the first time that whatever he saw had burrowed deep inside of him. "Nuh-uh," he said quietly. "It wasn't just a story."

] [

When the weekend hit, we acted like zombies—reanimated with routine. I told my parents I was going to meet the guys at the park to play basketball, but when I got on my bike, my legs were too leaden to pedal. Each movement took exceptional effort and as I went down the street away from my house, I dared not look back. I knew that Mom and Dad would be standing there, observing any imperfection in my exit, making note of it for reasons I'd never be able to understand.

I did not want to meet my friends. I did not want to play basketball. I only wanted to escape the terrible atmosphere of my own home, where my family's implacable double-talk had started to form the infrastructure of a lifelong neurosis.

"Just going out with the fellows, then?" asked Dad.

"Come home when the street lights come on. We'll be here, the two of us," said Mom.

The further I got away from home, the safer I felt. But then I passed by a row of houses.

The roar of an ancient engine. A jagged, stuttering, industrial cough.

My hands almost slipped off the handlebars.

I pedaled harder.

Just lawnmowers, I told myself. *They're just mowing their lawns.*

I flew down the street, a speck of light. Pure motion-blur. Slick with sweat, I outran the rumble. It faded into the distance, a faint growl, and as it quieted, I felt tension leave me.

It's going to be okay. Everything is fine, I thought.

When I got to the park, I threw my bike to the ground and fell into the grass, its cool blades tickling the backs of my arms and neck. *Everything is fine*, I kept repeating. A part of me knew it wasn't. A part of me felt as if I were on the edge of a cliff, and I had been my whole life. I'd just never thought to notice before—this whole time—that my feet were half off the edge. It would only take a tap.

I closed my eyes. The guys would arrive any minute.

We would talk about our mission, our adventure.

Somewhere distantly: bike chains, the sound of tires on gravel.

I kept my eyes closed. They would be here soon and we'd have to talk about it. They would be here soon and we'd have to face the facts. We'd have to talk about the congregation, the fellowship, the machine. The weird looks. The barbed words. The tight lips. *They'd be here soon,* I realized, and that meant everything we talked about for the last week was true and that we were really going to do this, we were really going to go to that old factory and see them and we were really going to talk about it. *Good God! They were so close!*

Monday was coming.

] [

I was lying in my bed, wide awake. This was my last chance to bail, I knew. My parents had eaten dinner at home that night, so obviously they were not going to go anywhere. I stared at the ceiling, hoping that everything was the same— that they too would be in bed sleeping and I was just letting myself get spooked. I was just a kid, a scared little kid. I thought I was older, bigger than I was, but suddenly, I was more than willing to be a mewling child.

Out of the corner of my eye, the red digits of my alarm clock blinked at me. My body went rigid. I could hear them.

Footsteps.

The creaking sound of floorboards sent bolts of shivers through my body. In my head I was screaming: *NO NO NO NO NO!*

My door opened, softly. The click of the lock, the soft push on greased hinges—I stayed so still I was half afraid they'd think I was dead.

But they just stood there. They did not speak. None of us moved a muscle.

I was counting seconds in my head. *One, two, three . . .*

They breathed softly, coolly. They were predators. They were waiting.

Sixteen, seventeen, eighteen . . .

I kept counting, my eyes shut tight, my teeth grinding. I imagined them, Mom and Dad—blank faces shrouded in shadows in my doorway. I wondered if they were counting too.

Sixty-two, sixty-three, sixty-four.

Then:

Click. The door closed with a deft hand. Light footsteps traveled down the hall.

(Seventy-two, seventy-three . . .)

I kept my eyes closed, I listened for the door downstairs and finally, finally, I let out the stale air in my lungs and breathed.

My muscles went lax. I felt safe enough to open my eyes. I blinked away the blackness and on unsure feet, rose from my bed and stepped lightly to my window. Under the orange glow of street lamps, I saw Mom and Dad walking arm in arm. And they were not alone.

It was a mass exodus. Throngs of people walked in the middle of the street. They were everywhere. All along the block there were children like me, fast asleep as their parents left them alone to go to the factory.

I threw on my clothes and climbed over fences, running spritely through backyards. *It was all too easy*, I thought. Way too simple.

We arrived at the same time, on the far edge of the lot, three small shapes trying to make sense of their mission.

"We have to do it," said Joe. "We can't not know now. We could have before, if Gaspar hadn't said anything." He glared at him, real rage wetting his eyes. "But we can't go back now because we do know. Gaspar told us and he ruined everything so now we have to go and see."

I pushed Gaspar, just lightly. "This is all your fault," I said. I didn't know where this anger was coming from, but it had been there since morning.

We hunkered down behind an old car and watched them go in, a single-file procession of deathly sobriety. I was still angry, upset at our being here. I think Joe was too. His fingers picked at the rusted metal of the car, removing chips of brown rust and letting them fall like snowflakes to the ground. Gaspar didn't do much of anything though, and that's why I didn't say anything more. I think he was taking it worse than any of us, as though—slowly—his reality had been dismantled. It had taken all week for him to understand the implications, but now his wide-eyed innocence was dead, bleeding out in the shadow of the factory.

The factory had always been there. But always, for us, was no more than twelve years. Everything in our small town had been there forever, as far as we were concerned. But this factory, somehow, seemed to have been here longer still than forever. It was a simple warehouse-looking building, a big box with rows of windows lining its three floors. Over time, it'd taken on a sickly green patina. The factory was a common place for kids to play. We'd surely been there at least a dozen times. Inside, it was empty except for detritus— sheets of plywood, crumbles of plaster, and exposed piping. Stairs ran along the wall to the next level, and from the that level onto the next. Sometimes, we'd hear about someone getting hurt there, or dying.

Now, years later, I think that's the strangest part of all. No one ever told us once not to play at the factory.

We strained our eyes against the darkness. "Are they all in?" whispered Joe.

"I think so," said Gaspar.

We ran across the lot, tip-toeing to the door. It was already half ajar, exposing perfect blackness.

We listened.

While this fellowship was undoubtedly quiet, we could still hear their clanging footsteps as they went up the metal stairs.

"Second floor," I said. Even outside, we could hear the floor above creak.

Then, fainter still, more clanging.

"They're up," said Gaspar.

"Let's go," said Joe.

He pushed the door open, deftly inserting himself into that impenetrable blackness. Gaspar followed, and so did I, holding my breath as if I were going underwater.

The factory smelled old, ancient. Like bone dust and salt water. On the inside, we could hear it. It was impossibly loud, steam pistons jackhammering, the screaming roar of an engine. It was as if an echo of the factory remained, a ghost of manufacturing past.

We could barely see, but our hands followed the sides of the wall and we found the stairs. Soon, we were climbing into a faint green glow that permeated the second floor.

Squinting, I took in my surroundings. Above us, the engine continued to sputter.

"I think they're doing it," said Gaspar in the faintest whisper. "I think they're—they're—"

We all knew what he wanted to say. *Praying.*

In the week since this revelation, the idea of prayer had been rendered grotesque to us, some sort of animal shame, like voiding one's bowels or striking a loved one. It was fitting that something so shameful would be done here, in the old factory.

Overcome with a sort of moral superiority—self-righteous anger at my parents and their failings—I urged my friends forward. "We're going to catch them in the act," I said.

I stood at the bottom step, staring up. The glow was more intense, but also murky. It was the black from old tinted photographs, where a shadow could be both emerald and opaque. I took my first step up and became suddenly wracked with fear. I thought of turning back right then, but Joe and Gaspar were looking at me. I knew I couldn't back down. Not after being so sure. So I climbed the stairs right to the point that the top of my head was just grazing the air of the third floor. I looked back.

The two of them hadn't moved.

I waved them forward. *C'mon!* I mouthed.

Dutifully, Joe, then Gaspar, followed me. Soon, we were all cramped on the stairs, three boys scared out of our minds, heart pumping in our ears, afraid of our next move.

We listened to the arrhythmic clanks of the machine our parents loved so much. I took a step forward, a lump in my throat, because I wanted to know why.

None of them saw us when we arrived.

The third floor was vast—full of tangled wires that hung from its ceiling and half demolished walls that stood like upright shards of glass. I thought maybe they were cubicles at some point; that this was where, some indefinite time ago, people had worked.

Staring out across the glowing floor, we saw them— dressed in the same clothes they always wore, facing away from us, circling around the machine. Up here, on the third floor, the machine sent vibrations through our feet. They stood staring at it, all of them, completely oblivious to us.

We got closer, traipsing behind cubicle walls, to see the clearing in which they stood. I wanted to see what they saw. I wanted to know what they knew. But they were too tall and we were just kids.

Then, the grown-ups, in silent synchronicity, all got down on one knee and we could see the machine.

It was about the size of a cow—a rectangle of twisted metal that in parts glowed white, as if it were overheating to its melting point. I wasn't sure how it was assembled, not really, but it looked like a bouquet of serpentine pipes, knotted together. It bucked back and forth, hissing steam and growling. It was hard for me not to think of it as alive.

Well, almost alive. Or rather, nearly not-alive.

Seeing it there, worshiped by this fellowship, I had the idea that this machine was dying.

Everyone but us, it appeared, knew this as a fact. Watching them now, in silent prayer, I wasn't sure if this was worship or ceremony. Were they comforting this machine as it died a long and agonizing death? Were they offering it what little strength they had for it to go on?

Joe and I took a step back, standing tall, fully aware that we were seeing something that we shouldn't be seeing. But Gaspar walked forward.

I wanted to yell at him, to tell him to stay away from the machine because really, he shouldn't be near it. It wouldn't be good for him. The machine would end him, I knew. Not kill him, but end him. It would take who he was and put a period after his name and a part of his life would cease. His life would be split—between before and after.

Joe and I, I think we realized at the same time that we did not want to be the people we would be after we prayed to the machine. We did not want those people to be us. Seeing them there, our parents and teachers and neighbors kneeled before the screaming, rumbling beast, we knew that we were better off before. One day, we might have to know it. Maybe they would drag us and force us to watch its dying breaths, but we would go kicking and screaming, crying "No! No! No!"

Gaspar would go willingly though. Maybe he was tired of the mockery. Or maybe he couldn't stand not knowing.

My lips locked together. If I yelled for him I'd be trapped too. I'd be a different person. I'd be the person who knew the machine.

So, Joe and I just kind of walked away, back to the stairs. We didn't really realize we were doing it, but that's how it happened. Gaspar was walking the other way and I think we were already trying to forget him. Like, forget he was ever our friend.

In the green glow of the roaring engine, on the top floor of the factory, Gaspar walked amongst the fellowship. Hands reached out, and to our surprise, touched him so gently that I almost wanted to run back up and say, *"Wait, I'm here too."* They were welcoming him. They let him stay. He breathed in the machine's steam heat and kneeled.

] [

For the rest of the year, Joe and I sat on the swings and didn't talk about the factory. We held onto whatever kept us from *knowing*.

We didn't see Gaspar much anymore, but when we did, he looked older, sallow, weathered for his age. He no longer giggled. He didn't come bounding across the playground with new information and endless enthusiasm. Gaspar just was.

Sometimes though, we would see him speaking to teachers and neighbors, grim determination spread across his lips. He spoke to them in urgent hushed whispers and when he thought we weren't looking, he stole a glance toward the swing set, toward us, and smiled wickedly.

But we just tried not to notice. It's all we could do.

ELOU CARROLL

The last shafts of daylight stretch through the broken panes of the frosted glass door, and you stand just before the threshold, fists clenched on your too-long sleeves. Tina—wild, irresponsible, and frankly deviant—has already gone ahead. Somewhere in the near-dark of the sorting office, she rifles through envelopes and periodicals and mail-order catalogues. Out here, with the wind drawing goosebumps up the back of your neck, you try to convince yourself not to snap Tina in half.

It's a birthday present, she'd said, when she told you what she'd done, smiling all the while. *You always said you wanted to. There's no day like today!*

Then later, she'd said, *It's a small town. How many letters can there be? We'll be in and out in no time. It'll be like it never happened. Promise.*

Tina has never been good at keeping promises.

There's no day like today. That's what you tell yourself, imagining Tina's peppy not-a-care attitude as you push the door open and step inside, wincing at the glass that crunches out *shouldn't even be here*, in Morse code beneath your feet.

You always wanted an old telegraph machine, knew all of the codes and abbreviations, all of the first transmissions and lasts by heart—the first, *What hath God wrought?*, was the same thing you said when things went wrong, when Tina told you what she did.

As children, Tina and you had made do with torches, light in lieu of sound, dotting and dashing between your bedroom windows across the street where you both grew up. You bet they have one here, a telegraph machine—this place hasn't been updated in years. This is the side entrance, none of the usual polite reception desks and potted plants. Instead, it is a large warehouse filled with an eruption of mail cages and postal sacks, letters strewn hither and thither as if the order of the day had been the exact opposite of *sorting*. Along one wall, a row of giant rusted shutters, all of them closed—the only evidence that there is still a world outside is the door behind you. Even if you squint, in the dim green glow of the building's emergency lighting, the only glimmer of modernity, you can't see the back wall. This place could go on forever.

You should be in Paris, or at least on your way. Somewhere beneath the Channel, pretending you can see fish, when really it's just tunnel. But then, Paris.

You swing the wind-up torch from side to side—the one you keep in your car for emergencies, and *this* definitely constitutes an emergency. The beam is a sickly thing, but it'll have to do.

"Tina, found it yet?" The words echo and yet, at the same time, sound is muffled, like there's water pooled in your ear canal, like you're in the tunnel and the tunnel is leaking.

No answer comes.

She's supposed to be looking for letters stuffed into brown paper envelopes, but Tina is probably head-first in a parcel bin. Always an eye for opportunity, that one. That's what got you into this mess in the first place. Tina is probably having an excellent time.

It's not *just* Tina's fault, she didn't write the letters. You never would have, if you'd known. One to your mother, who you've not seen for the last five years; another to your boss, a weaselly twit of a man who'd sooner see you kicked out of your digs than ever pay you on time; and a third to 'the one that got away'. Each of them a dam fit to burst and rush your world—your life—to pieces.

You should have stuck to postcards—the kind that say *Wish You Were Here* without actually meaning it.

"Is this really what you want?" The sound is full of stops and starts, the Morse code of the glass under your boots made vocal, made into words. You, too, stop, the words punching holes in your bones.

The voice comes from deeper in the building, where the waning window light doesn't reach.

"Tina?" you ask, because it has to be Tina. There's no one else here, and though it lacks her liquid lilt, it cannot possibly be anyone else.

Again, she doesn't reply.

Prosign **NIL**: *Nothing Heard.*

In fact, there is no sound at all now. Not the rustling of paper or the moving of boxes, not even the tiny hum of the barely-lit emergency lights.

"This isn't funny, Tina."

Still nothing. You manoeuvre around a mail cart and—*yes, there*—even the sound of your footsteps is swallowed until they are barely louder than the dot-dot-dot, dash-dash-dash, dot-dot-dotting of your heart.

Prosign **SOS**: *Start of a Distress Signal.*

Up ahead, something moves.

Your heartbeat catches in your throat.

"Tina, wait!" you say, because it has to be Tina, just like the voice.

You don't stop to search as you move through the sorting office—that can be done *after* you've throttled Tina, she *knows* you don't like the dark. Don't like being *alone* in the dark. Still, you're careful not to disturb these snail mail mountains, hunched in the dark like creatures waiting.

Watching.

You feel it in the back of your neck, the sensation of something looking, *really* looking, but when you turn your head, of course there's nothing there.

"Is this really what you want?"

The voice is closer now. It could be right behind you, or just up ahead. The sound swallowed and regurgitated between paper and card and packing tape. You're being stupid, and the just-downed sun is playing tricks on you— *Tina* is playing tricks on you. Who else could it be? There's something of her lilt to it, afterall. Isn't there?

"You can come out now. You've got me. I'm scared. You win."

When she doesn't emerge, you trudge still deeper. It's bigger in here than it looks from the outside. Rows and rows of pigeonholes stretch amid the carts and cages, disappearing into the dark. A few of them contain neat bundles of post, ready for the morning rounds, but the rest are either empty or damaged, as if something ripped away their contents with hands too big, too strong, too sharp.

A figure sways down the central aisle. Too far away for your little torch to light them.

You swallow. In the green emergency light, you could be seeing a person where there is only a misshapen pile of parcels. Maybe it's not moving at all. The dark can do that.

Or it could be—

"Tina, I swear to God . . ."

The figure stops.

Turns.

Is not Tina.

Says, "Is this really what you want?"

You should stop. The telegraph is finished. You shouldn't get any closer to—whoever this is. The telegraph is in and it's telling you to leave. You should find Tina and *go*.

But you can't. Not until you've found the letters.

You don't mean to walk towards the figure, but there's something spurring you forward—a shove at your back that you can't place.

"Is this *really* what you want?"

This time, the voice is familiar. Tinny and rippling and wrong, like it's coming across a tannoy deep beneath the sea, like it's been recorded and played back at not quite the right pitch, but still, it's unmistakable.

You're close now—too close. So near you could lean forward, reach out your hand, and touch them.

In the meagre torchlight, you see their—*your*—face. Forget to breathe. The you that stands opposite is *wrong* in a way that you can't put your finger on, like looking through water, though they wear the clothes that you do, their hair is styled just like yours is. You run your fingers across your lips, your eyes, your eyebrows—even their expression is an echo of your own.

That's the thing with echoes, they never come back quite right.

They step forwards as you step back, accidentally kicking a tape gun so that it skitters across the walkway like a frightened animal: dot-dash, dot-dot-dot, it says.

Prosign **AS**: *Stand By.*

Tina. Where the hell are you? Your gaze thrashes from side to side, desperate to catch a glimpse of her slipping between parcel cages, desperate to find her and grab her and run. This thing can have the letters, you can live with the consequences, assuming you live at all.

Morbid much? That's what Tina would say.

Tina is probably already in Paris.

It'd be just like her to leave you here, but to do that, she would have had to pass you—and you've not seen her since she slipped through the broken door.

The echo walks slowly, never blinking and always with the question: *is this really what you want?* They do not rush. Their hands reach towards you, creeping out like kelp in water, but you don't want to know what would happen if they manage to touch you.

They're so close to touching you.

You back away from their slow approach, trying desperately not to fall. You've never been coordinated, especially not in dark, unfamiliar, frankly, terrifying places. Each step you take feels heavy, like wading through mud. If the same is true of the echo, they don't show it. For them, walking looks easy, effortless. More like gliding.

The echo is gaining on you.

You don't want to look away from them, but they'll catch you if you don't *hurry up,* and you certainly can't run backwards. The moment you turn away, their steps come quicker, their questioning more urgent.

So you run.

You run, and the sorting office seems to tunnel out in front of you. For every pace you gain, ten more spread between you and the door. You step on a plastic-wrapped catalogue and it slides beneath your foot, sending you sprawling. Your chin crashes into the cold tile and you hiss, your teeth sinking into your bottom lip.

You scramble to your feet just as a hand brushes your coat. For a moment you are outside yourself, looking down as if from above. Then, in a blink, you are looking *at* yourself—the real you, the you that is running, the you that is no longer.

The echo's hand—no, *your* hand—clenches on the coat.

They smile, and an *is this really what you want?* slips from the mouth that used to be yours.

No, you want to say. *No, no, no.* But your new mouth doesn't work right. All it spits is plosive dots and breathy dashes. You try to tug them back by your coat, but they just shrug and let it slide off into your hand. You can't let them do this. You won't let them do this. *This* isn't what you want.

But the echo walks easier in your shoes, fits better in your skin. Their steps are light. You can't see their—your—face anymore, but you know that they're smiling. You can feel that smile pantomiming on the face they've left you with.

You try to run, but *they're* not running and so neither do you. You're never going to catch them. They don't *want* you to catch them.

Is this what you really want? Their words come to you unbidden, and for a moment, you think you might understand them—you think you might have said it yourself, before. Might always have been them, might always have been this.

You could let them go. You could let them live in the mess that Tina created—the mess you let Tina create. You could. You could.

You can't.

Trying to run is fruitless, but you do it anyway. You do it until you scream, if only you could.

But they reach the door before you do.

Of course they do.

You stand on the threshold, fists clenched on your too-long sleeves. Tina—impulsive, wonderful, stupid Tina—is waiting outside. Out there, the you that you were goes to her without a backward glance.

"What took you so long? I've been waiting for you." She doesn't wait for an answer before she flashes three brown envelopes, smiling all the while. "See, told you. Easy."

The you that you were plucks the letters from her hand. "You know what?" They push the letters back into the postbox, consequences be damned, and smile right back at her. "Screw it. Paris, here we come."

"Is this really what you want?" Tina asks, and they shrug.

You want to burst through the broken door, or hammer on it with your fists.

Prosign **KA**: *Attention.*

But all you can do is echo their smile. The first shafts of moonlight stretch through the broken panes in the sorting office door, and you stand on the threshold, watching yourself leave.

With your finger, you trace a telegraph, the last one sent by the French Navy and the first one sent in your lifetime, the day you—*they*—were born.

-.-. .- .-.. .-.. .. -. --. / .- .-.. .-.. .-.- /

Calling all.

.-.-. -.-. .- .-.. .-.. .. -. --. / .- .-.. .-.. .-.- / - .... / .. ... / --- ..- .-.
/ .-.. .- ... - / -.-. .-. -.-- / -.... . ..-. --- .-. . / --- ..- .-. / . - .-. -. .- .-.. /
... .. .-.. . -. -.-. . .-.-. .-.-.

This is our last cry before our eternal silence.

the hole had always been there

REBECCA CUTHBERT

The hole in the retaining wall had always been there, as far back into the *before* as Davey could remember.

The earth it held back sloped up and away from Davey's yard, rising into a hill.

Beyond the hill lay the cemetery.

Davey's mom was there now, and her now meant *forever*. She would *always now* be there, while he was stuck, helpless, in the *after*.

] [

Hours after his mother's funeral, Davey stood near the retaining wall, hidden by the garage, smoking a joint he'd filched from his father. Not that his dad was likely to notice—neither Davey being gone, nor the missing joint—because Davey's father was in a fog of grief and bewilderment and noticed nothing.

Davey was on his own.

He stared at the hole in the wall and tried not to shiver in the March wind. He was a "tough kid"—the term everyone seemed to be using for him, which, Davey knew, translated to "kid with a dead mom."

But tough kids get cold too and Davey *did* shiver, huddling closer to the tight-packed stones that made up the retaining wall. Closer to the hole.

It seemed bigger than it used to be.

Was it the angle? Davey moved away—no. It *was* bigger, though wasn't *bigger* a funny way to describe a hole? *Bigger* meant *substance*; *bigger* meant *bulk*. A hole was an *absence*; a hole was a lack, and the only thing Davey could think about now was what he lacked.

Thinking and brooding, trying not to shiver or cry, Davey wrapped his lips around the joint and sucked its skunky fug into his lungs. Thanks to his eleventh-grade health class, he knew all about weed's dangers: *naphthalene, acrylamide, acrylonitrile metabolites*. He whispered the names of the poisons and inhaled again. Like a magic spell, they rode the smoke into all the places within himself Davey could not see—dark, empty places hollowed by grief—and filled them up.

He leaned forward and blew smoke into the hole.

The hole blew it back.

Davey's eyes watered and stung. He coughed.

Then, curious, he stepped closer, looking for the source of the air current. Wind through a drainage pipe? Maybe an animal's den—a fox or raccoon, huffing Davey's smoke back and away?

Poking into the hole seemed dangerous—*foolish*, his mother would have said, but she was dead and couldn't scold him about this (or anything else) ever again.

Davey put his hand in first, then his arm up to the elbow. Inside it was chilly and still. No wind moved, no animal scuttled. The space was large—larger than its mouth, though even that was growing again, widening, as if the retaining wall was yawning. Davey heard the sound of rocks rubbing together within the hole's black nothing. It made him think of cracking bones.

He knew holes shouldn't shift and grow this way. But he thought he'd known that mothers didn't fall down dead without warning. Here, in the *after*, Davey understood the rules of the *before* were meaningless—dirty tricks played on little boys who didn't know better but would soon enough.

He pulled his hand out and watched. The hole dilated. Loose dirt sifted down to the grass, dislodged by the heaving and grinding of the stones. Davey wondered if the wall would crumble—if the hill would come sliding down, burying the yard and the garage and Davey with them, rolling over him like a dark drowning wave of clammy earth.

He wondered if he would like it. He thought he might.

The sounds stopped.

The hole didn't grow any larger.

He measured the opening: a diameter longer than his forearm. If he squeezed through, he could crawl inside. If he crawled inside, the rest of the lonely, motherless world would go away. And if the rest of the world went away, Davey could finally cry, as long and hard and as hopelessly as he wanted.

He went in.

As his foot left the security of his lawn, Davey wondered if his father had eaten anything for dinner. He often forgot, and wouldn't eat unless Davey microwaved something and set it down in front of him—reheated casseroles left by the neighbors, or frozen Hungry Man meals bought on sale.

It made him ache to worry about his dad, and he worried about him all the time.

He told himself he'd return to his dad soon—but not yet.

The dirt he knelt in was soft, and Davey reached out with his right hand to explore the rest of his surroundings: damp earth and hair-thin roots. Here and there, a smooth pebble.

The tip of his joint gave off no light. He pulled his knees up and sat, careful not to crush the wriggling, wet body of a night crawler his knuckle brushed against.

He squeezed his eyes shut and told himself it would be fine to cry. He wanted to cry. He always wanted to cry. But he was tired. So tired that sitting seemed difficult. So he leaned back and stubbed out his joint, enjoying the way it hissed in the dirt, enjoying the way the dirt cradled his body.

Then he heard his father calling him from the back porch. His voice sounded raw; the second time he said Davey's name, it cracked.

Davey knew he should call back. Tell his dad he was okay; go to him, microwave something, sit next to him on the couch. Eat and pretend to watch tv and then go to bed, telling himself that if nothing else—and there was nothing else—they had each other. Or at least, Davey's dad had him.

He looked back toward his house; he opened his mouth to holler.

The hole's mouth shrank.

Davey's jaw clamped shut; his lips pinched together in a thin, worried line. The hole shrank again.

He pitched himself forward to crawl out—he'd claw through if he had to—but a new sound made him stop.

It came from deeper within the hole—from deep within the place the hole led to—from shadows and root-twists and dankness and a breeze like warm breath: his mother's voice.

Come here, sweetheart.

Her tone was the same as always, the same as when she'd needed him—to come in for dinner, to help her in the garden, to tell her about the book he was reading.

Hearing it again took all the oxygen from his lungs. He sat back.

"Mom?" he whispered.

Then a call from the other direction—his dad's voice: "Davey? Are you there?" Louder and closer. In the backyard now, shouting from the darkness near the rusted swingset he'd built for Davey more than ten years ago.

Davey was torn.

He could smell his mother—plain Dove soap and rosemary sap.

Honey? her voice said.

"Mom."

"Davey?" his dad called. A note of panic pitched his voice high: "Son!"

Was his mother humming? She used to—old songs Davey didn't know.

His chest tightened. He wanted to crawl out and he wanted to crawl deeper.

His mother's voice called him: *Davey!*

His father's voice called him: "Davey!"

He missed them both—his mother who was gone forever; his father, who was gone too, in a different way.

His mother's voice called to him: *Come here, sweetheart.*

His father's voice called to him: "Come on! It's late."

He loved them both. He missed them both.

He couldn't do it anymore.

The tight feeling in his chest gave way to a tearing; something inside pulled to the outside, like stuffing ripped out of a plush toy.

Davey went cold, then hot—a flush from the top of his spine to his heels. Bright, sharp pain, so quick he couldn't scream, gone just as fast, its departure like bubbles rising, leaving him dizzy.

Then, dreamlike, he watched himself frown, turn away, and crawl toward the mouth of the tunnel, toward his father's voice. His head and then arms and then shoulders and waist and hips legs feet disappeared. He heard his dad's voice—he called him, the other Davey, "buddy."

His dad said, "There you are!" He said, "Let's go inside."

And that other Davey must have said a word like "yes," or "okay," or even a sulky "fine," because then Davey—the Davey still inside the hole—didn't hear anything more.

Until he did.

A *different* sound.

It was his mother's laugh—the delighted one, like when she won a game of Scrabble or knew the answer on *Wheel of Fortune.* The voice box in his very own throat croaked out "Mom?"

Then her laugh again, like confirmation, like Come closer. So he yelled it: "Mom!"

He wondered if he was dead too.

He wondered if ghosts could feel sad.

He wondered if he should leave—hurry, catch up to his other self, stitch them back together, decide for good that *after* was better than not at all.

But: *Davey. Honey. Davey,* his mother's voice called. Quieter now. She was moving away from him—leaving him, again.

No.

He couldn't let that happen.

Without looking behind him, without looking at the gap that was a doorway that was salvation that was an escape that was the way back to his yard, back to his life, back to his dad, back to his grief—the opening the exit the hole that was maybe getting smaller even now, was maybe shrinking down to nothing and there'd be no undoing this, but Davey didn't care, he called again: "Mom!"

Davey?

"Wait!" he said. "Mom . . ."

The tunnel wound long, it wove through the dark, and he crawled and he crawled—this underworld Davey, this otherworld Davey, already so pale—he crawled to his mother and into her arms; her arms felt so cold, the cold chilled so deep; in the deep-dark they stayed and there they lay still.

Always, now.

Always, ever after.

glass door

Ivy Grimes

Before the service, Lane sat alone in the nicest room in the funeral parlor. It was also the smallest room, with a plush red carpet and display of fake roses. She felt a panic coming on, so she needed solitude and the room's eerie calm. She'd poured herself coffee in the kitchen since that was what all the adults were doing, and at fourteen, she felt it was time to take sides. Her little cousins were all playing on the lawn with her stepdad, and she was obviously too old for that. Her family had laughed at her, like they would have done anyway.

"Coffee at your age?" Uncle Matt had said. "Do you think you're grown already? It's a bad habit. That's what it is."

Aunt Dee had taken her aside and said, "I know you think coffee makes you thin, but really, it'll make you fat. I just have to warn you. It increases your sugar cravings because the caffeine molecules bind to your stomach acid in a fat-loving way. I read a book about it."

What was she supposed to say to that? She did like coffee, she thought, but she *really* liked frappuccinos. The funeral coffee tasted like bile, though once she'd asked for her own styrofoam cupful, she had to pretend she didn't mind.

Lane sipped without grimacing while her aunts and uncles kept talking, and she would have acted fine if she hadn't heard Aunt Lila whisper to her mom: "I don't know what Lane's going to do without her Grandma. I hope it doesn't lead to any of that trouble again."

She'd asked her mom not to tell anyone about her "trouble," but she'd been betrayed, as usual. Why had she trusted her mom? Her own family couldn't even wait until she wasn't in the same room to gossip about her. They were glad she'd tried to kill herself, as long as it gave them something to chat about. Lane kept still for a minute, like she didn't care, before sneaking away to find some peace and quiet.

Everyone in her family who died had a service in Day's Funeral Home, followed by another at graveside, in West Park Cemetery, right beside it. One day, she'd have hers there too, unless something happened. Something that took her far away, or something that made her unsuitable for the place.

A full-length mirror with a golden frame took up one little wall in the parlor, set up for mourners to check their black outfits, or to see if their mascara was running. Lane went up to it to put on some lipstick from a tube she'd hidden in her skirt pocket, something she thought might soothe her. It would be pretty to leave a little red stain on the styrofoam cup, too.

The lipstick went on in its chalky way, but soon she was distracted by a change. One second she was watching her own lips, and the next she couldn't see herself. The glass had frosted over. And something else. There was movement behind the glass, a shadow that crept close to her.

Who was it? Grandma, was her first thought. She was willing to crawl through glass to see Grandma again. In the corner of the mirror, she saw a glass doorknob. It was vital to see what was on the other side, so she grabbed the knob, expecting it to be cold to the touch. Instead, it was warm, like flesh.

When she twisted the glass doorknob, it broke in her hands, shattering the whole mirror silently. It sounded like a scream so high only dogs could hear it, but Lane could hear it, too. The funeral home would probably charge her family an extra thousand dollars for breaking that beautiful mirror. And think of all the bad luck.

The door cracked open, though. The knob had been pinning it shut, but now that it was broken, she might as well pass through. They could all go to hell, but she was going sideways. She had to get away from all of them.

Afraid that the frosted glass would shatter if she pushed too hard, she squeezed through the small opening. On some level, she still thought of the door as a mirror, and she expected to see some version of the funeral parlor on the other side.

Instead, there was a great white room with hard tile, waiting chairs, and a television in the corner. This was a place she knew, the hospital she'd been to on four occasions. Once for her Grandma and three times for herself. Two of those times, she didn't even have to wait.

There were people there: a receptionist behind a desk, and several people sitting in plastic chairs as far apart from each other as possible.

"How can I help you?" the receptionist said.

Lane approached the desk and examined the receptionist for signs of ghostliness. "I don't know," Lane said. "There was a door, so I went through it."

She thought she saw a familiar face out of the corner of her eye. It was on the television. When she looked up, she saw her grandma on-screen, lying in her pink satin casket, her eyes closed, her cheeks rouged. At rest.

"Why is that on television?" Lane said.

The receptionist looked concerned, which was how adults often looked around her, and Lane began to wish she hadn't come. She didn't belong in this place any more than she had in the other.

"She's with me," a woman behind her said.

When Lane turned to see who it was, she found herself, but one who was older and a little taller. Grown. Short blue hair and tattoos, just like she wanted to look.

"Come sit with me," she said, then took Lane's hand and led her to the far corner of the waiting room.

"Are you me?" Lane said.

"Well, I don't know. Are you the same person you were when you were four?"

"I guess not. Or maybe so."

"Then you see why it's hard to answer. Anyway, it doesn't matter. Think of me as someone else if it helps. I'm the one who brought you here."

"Why?" Lane said.

"To protect you."

The receptionist turned up the TV, and the funeral began with some organ music, "How Great Thou Art."

"Why is this on TV? Is Grandma famous here?" she said.

"It's happening," the receptionist whispered. Tears filled her eyes, and she pulled a box of tissues out of her deep desk drawer.

Unable to move, Lane kept watching as the camera panned closer to her grandma's set face, her puffy eyelids. She wished Grandma could open her eyes once more. She had such kind eyes.

As the hymn finished, the camera pulled back to show the coffin from a distance. The pastor stood before it and said, "God bless this woman."

"I don't want to watch!" Lane cried out, shrieking a little. "I don't want to!"

Everyone in the room ignored her except her older self, who put her hand over Lane's eyes.

"I can still hear," Lane whimpered. The pastor was saying a few words about her Grandma's life, about her charity work and family, her beautiful garden. She tried to think of something else to take her mind off of it, but all she could think about was being at the ER. In the back of the hospital, it was all right, because they gave you something that made you feel better. Being in the waiting room, though, meant trying to hold your own broken pieces together and it was enough to make her wish she didn't have to live.

"Think of something else," Older Lane said. "Think of the pool party where they had those swan floats."

She tried to imagine herself as a little kid, clambering on the plastic white float, slipping off into the water. She'd laughed and laughed.

"How are you protecting me here?"

Older Lane pulled out a cigarette and lit it, and somehow no one objected. The receptionist was glued to the funeral, in awe of the humble affair.

"Look at those diamonds," the receptionist kept saying, though Lane didn't know which diamonds she was talking about. Maybe some jewelry that belonged to her aunts. Her grandma had given Aunt Lila her engagement ring.

"I'm getting your mind off things. There are some things that'll kill you if you think about them too much. You already know that."

Lane looked down at her hands. She was still wearing her black funeral dress and the silver bracelet her Grandma had given her for Christmas. Her Grandma had said, *Even when you think no one loves you, remember that I love you.*

"Don't think about that. Not right now," Older Lane said. She finished her cigarette and crunched it under her boot, left it on the hospital floor.

"I would have been okay at the funeral."

Older Lane looked at her like she was insane. "I'm not overreacting here. I know things. Anyway, something happens in that room you were in. It's better you wait here with me."

"Why are you here?"

"Something's going on out there. For me. You wouldn't understand right now."

As the service progressed, it came time for each family member to approach the open casket for their final goodbyes.

The receptionist went from dabbing at her eyes to sobbing into a wad of tissues.

To Lane's surprise, she saw herself on TV, in the procession line. She was there, in the service, and through the glass at the same time.

"My hair looks messy," Lane said to her older self.

Older Lane fluffed her blue hair, as if to say she'd found the answer.

When TV Lane reached the casket, she let her head drop into it. It was too long for a kiss goodbye. Someone had to pull her out. Her mom. Her stepdad. The pastor stood nearby and looked embarrassed for her.

The receptionist watched it all in awe and shouted out in pity for her. "That poor girl. That poor girl!"

Lane couldn't take it anymore. She stood up and walked. Voices shouted after her, but she ran, back the way she came in. She had to return to the other side of the glass so she could run away, go home while everyone was at the funeral potluck, pack her bags, buy a bus ticket to somewhere far away.

When she returned to the glass door, the full-length frosted mirror, she tried to look through it, into the funeral parlor. Was she really at the funeral, or was she still there in that hospital waiting room?

She could only see shadows, but she could see that someone was sitting in the chair where she'd sat. Some shadow. Above the chair stood another shadow.

"I have to do something," Lane said. "I have to go back."

There was a glass knob on that side of the door, too, and she broke it. She knew she couldn't leave without breaking the knob, and who knew when the knob would reappear? It was dangerous both to go and to stay, but she squeezed herself through the opening and returned to the funeral room.

She saw herself sitting in her old chair, bawling her eyes out. She closed her eyes and found herself in her own body again, which was heaving with some misery. She tried and tried to think, but she couldn't remember why she was crying. Her Grandma was dead, but it wasn't just that. Something had happened, or someone had said something to her. Maybe it was kind of her older self to have retrieved her, to have helped her forget. Something was said or something was done. Where could she go if she ever wanted to get the memory back? Maybe she'd find another mirror, another glass knob, another glass door.

Her mom walked into the room and told her to calm down. She said it in a nice way, but still, it was impossible.

"I know you loved your Grandma," her mom said. "I loved her too. I'm so sorry she's gone."

Lane was crying too hard to say anything. Lipstick was smeared on her hand. She heard voices in the parking lot, some too joyful for the occasion.

"When does it start?" she said. At least she'd get to be there for the funeral.

"It's all over now. Thank you for waiting here while we had the graveside. You just weren't up for it, hon. Now, as soon as you're ready, we're just going to drive right down the road to Aunt Lila's so we can all have lunch together. Oh, I'm so sorry, Lane. No one blames you for having a hard time saying goodbye."

The service was over. She'd seen all she would ever see of it on that television. The receptionist had cried for her. She would never have the chance to be in her own body, shedding her own tears when she told her Grandma goodbye.

Maybe Older Lane was right. Maybe it was better not to think about it. Lane looked up at her dry-eyed mom, took a deep breath, and promised to wash her face in the bathroom.

At least now she knew. She knew there was an Older Lane, that some Lane would survive. And she knew there was a place to go when something bad happened. It wasn't a beautiful place or a peaceful place, but it was somewhere sideways. All she had to do was look hard in the mirror, and the doorway might appear.

queue

Julie Sevens

Joe shook his water bottle, half-heartedly looking around
for a fountain. "How long you think this'll take?" he asked.
He pulled the travel pillow from his stiff neck and tucked it
into his luggage.

"You're worried we won't make the train." Bean was
debating over the placement of another sticker--a hot pink
palm tree she'd bought from a street vendor on the drunken
walk home from a foam party in Ibiza—and didn't look up.
Finally, she smoothed it down onto the onion-layers of other
stickers clinging to her laptop.

"Well, we haven't moved in almost an hour."

Twenty minutes ago, they'd plunked themselves down
against a softly rattling radiator box at the end of the line.
New people had joined since then, crushing in behind them

as they flowed from the capillaries of jetways into this main artery through customs, but there was a stubborn clot of people ahead. The line behind them only grew longer.

Bean snorted. "That's just how it is. You know that. It's always like this. Four hours, minimum."

Joe put his trusty old Samsonite—inherited from his dad, down to the aftershave scent in the silky blue lining—on the floor, and stood on top of it. The hard shell creaked like elderly bones but only dented a little under his weight.

The snake of people in the customs line went so far ahead of them, Joe couldn't see the front.

He could feel Bean looking at him with that withering eyebrow raised. "Like I said, you know, it takes forever. That's why I made you pee on the plane even though you whined about it, Seff. Also why we left so much room in our schedule before the train." She shrugged. "But even if we miss it, they'll let us on a later one. We'll just lose our seat reservation."

"I hate it when you call me Seff. We're not nine anymore."

A ripple moved through the crowd, as if an invisible searchlight was passing over, and a wave of dread permeated Joe's bones. It was followed by a whisper, or maybe a silence—a change in volume, somehow.

Bean put away her laptop and picked at the industrial gray carpet fibers. The square by her fingers peeled up at the corner, slapping back down against the adhesive-mottled cement beneath.

She sighed and pulled out two foil-packeted granola bars that she somehow still had from home, even after all their time away.

"Did you feel that?" Inside his brain felt like static, a hum of anxiety, a change in the air.

"Eat this, you're getting weird."

The line moved, and they crunched up the empty wrappers, stuffing them in their pockets, crumbs sprinkling the carpet. Five feet at first. Then ten. Then the snake slithered along and drew Bean and Joe away from the wall, into the line, further and further.

Joe skimmed his hand along the black rope of the stanchions, patting each silver post in turn. Then they got to a turn, and Bean's roller bag tipped over as she tried to maneuver it. More turns, more posts.

"Finally getting somewhere," Joe said. The minute he opened his mouth, the people in front of them stopped. Bean crashed into his heels.

"See?" One eyebrow was up, her 'told you so' expression.

"We stopped moving, dork."

"Yeah but we moved! Do you want to play blackjack or something? Rock Paper Scissors?" She'd always been good at distracting him from unpleasantness.

"We're going to move again, I bet."

Bean pulled her laptop from her bag and picked at the corner of one of the stickers she'd put on earlier, giving up when it wouldn't peel.

They were stuck under the cone of a light that flickered on and off, staccato, strobing. Joe wondered if he could hit it with something to make it stop. It was irritating him, more than it should. Maybe he was hangry.

He scratched the back of his head, flexed his shoulders. Finished the water in his bottle and fiddled with the cap. He was taut, a guitar string pulled away from the frets, ready to snap.

Joe chucked his empty water bottle at the blinking light. It pinged off the metal cone and a water droplet hit him in the face. The woman behind them tutted in annoyance.

The light blinked faster and made a humming noise.

"What the hell are you doing, Joe?"

"Something's weird, Bean. This line is too long." The flickering light swayed gently.

By the next time they inchwormed along, Joe was sweating. It was a sticky, instantly damp sweat. The tag on the back of his shirt started itching.

He tried to resist standing on his suitcase again, but after a moment, he kicked it over and stepped up on it anyway.

"I can't see the walls anymore."

Bean laughed.

"I'm fucking serious. There's no end. The line just keeps going. I can't even see the door where we came in. The ceiling just goes and goes. Look."

Bean refused to look. "You did this in Frankfurt too. Remember? And Newark before that. You are bad at lines, Seff. Just like Mom."

"I said, stop calling me Seff." Joe dug his fingernails into his palms. He sucked in a deep breath. This was irrational. Of course the line would end.

Everyone around him looked bored. None of them looked like their skin was melting off. All of them had mouths where they should be. The toddler in the family next to them giggled at someone playing peekaboo. This was just another line in another airport. They would make their train.

Bean patted his arm.

The toddler got further away, carried deeper into the maze. The line was moving again. Joe breathed in, the sweat cooling against his skin. He nodded. They walked on through the maze of ropes and posts.

The tops of a row of booths appeared through the crowd, several rows over, white caps over sliding glass windows. A few more times around bends, a few more long walks down and back in the hall that didn't end, and they'd be out.

"See," Bean said, nudging him. "Almost there. You got your passport out?"

Joe and Bean slogged along the next row, then the next, then the next. He imagined the crisp air that would blast his face as he left the airport; impossibly fresh even in the pickup lane, that first breath outdoors after a day on planes and in airports.

The line shuffled to a stop again, after Joe counted five times that they'd reached the end of a row and looped back around. They should be five rows closer to the booths.

"I thought we'd be almost to the end by now," Joe said.

"Do you have any water left?" she asked him.

He shook his head. "I threw it at the light, 'member?" The rows of metal cones, pendant lights that cast a net of green-tinted shadows, hung silently. The light above them flickered lazily, forgetting to turn back on for seconds at a time.

Joe looked behind them for the other flickering light, wondering how far they'd come. "Where is that stupid light anyway? It should be back there somewhere."

Bean's foot kicked a water bottle with a peeling label. It pinged against the closest post, drips of water rolling down the inside of the blue plastic. She picked it up and held it out to him.

"You dropped your water bottle," Bean insisted when he didn't reach out to take it, bouncing the bottle closer to his chest.

"No. I threw it at the light. A while ago. Way back there." he jerked his thumb over his shoulder. "You really don't remember?"

"Well, this is yours. Look, see?" She pointed at the worn-away name, Sharpied on the bottom.

Joe put his carry-on on the ground, stacked his backpack on top of it, then snatched Bean's bags too, to add height. He ignored her protests that her laptop was in the bag.

His shoes dug into the canvas folds and he found his balance as he struggled atop the makeshift pile. He couldn't find the entrance where they'd come in. The faraway edges of the line smudged into darkness where he'd expected the walls to be. Like looking into an infinity mirror.

"Bean. *Sabrina.* This line *doesn't end.*" Joe's foot slipped, and his ankle twisted painfully as he stepped back on the commercial carpet tiles. His breathing pulled at the tendons in his ribs.

The crowd behind them in the line inched forward, a nearly imperceptible movement. But Joe had seen that was an illusion; the line snaked this way, that way, turned around on itself, but not in the direction of any end.

As far as he could see, there was only more line. There was no *forward.*

"Look, it's almost done." She was pointing into the middle distance.

"Bean, we have to get out of here. This line never ends." He wanted to grab her and shake her, but she was staring at nothing, her eyes glazed. Lost. A smile hinted at the corners of her mouth, like the painted lips of a doll.

Joe felt like he had known which way should be the end, but he no longer could remember where he had expected the booths with the grumpy officers demanding everyone's passports to be. He couldn't get his bearings, couldn't decide where they'd been, or where they should be going.

He closed his eyes, tucked his head down, and breathed slowly, trying to stop the sick spinning that was developing deep in his body. The static in his head was louder, oppressive.

When he opened his eyes, Bean had continued five feet down the line. But when Joe caught up to her, she blinked at him blankly, coldly.

"Bean?" He touched her arm and she recoiled, then turned away, to keep shuffling on. Bodies bumped into him, softly, muffled cotton and wheely bags flowing around him like a lazy stream. The crowd swallowed her up. Joe tried to weave between the others, tried to get where he was going. Tried to remember his goal.

As he pressed forward, Joe wondered why he was sticky with sweat, why his heart was pounding. Had he been running? He'd been trying to catch up with someone, maybe. His pace slowed to match the people around him. *I'll catch up, I'm sure.*

His foot kicked a blue water bottle, and it rolled into a post under a flickering light. S-E-F-F was scrawled on it with marker. Joe wondered whose it was, why they'd dropped it.

Joe walked on. He must have a goal. We must all be going somewhere. His feet shuffled along behind the person in front of him. He passed post after post along a long black cordon. His finger skimmed a couple of posts, but his arm felt heavy and dropped to his side. Easier to focus on walking.

In a last blink of awareness, Joe imagined a lone, floating soap bubble, circling a drain.

out of context

ALEX WOLFGANG

"Do you think it would get old," Sarah asked, "Living in a bubble like this?"

Jeff stuffed an olive and a slice of manchego cheese into his mouth, blending it to a pulp with a sip of Czech wine. "A bubble?"

"Yeah." She leaned back on her blanket, propping herself up on her arms. "I just mean, it doesn't feel like we're in the real world."

The two sat against a fence beside a copse of trees, looking at the old, weathered gravestones near Vyšehrad Castle. It was an instance of good timing, when most of the other tourists had already made their way through the dimming evening toward Prague's pubs and restaurants. The place had been bustling half an hour ago, but the only evidence of this were footprints left in grass and dirt, softened by afternoon rain. Now there remained only a handful of onlookers, oohing and ahhing at the graves of famous Czechs. They paid no attention to Jeff and Sarah.

"I mean, it is the real world, though, right?" Jeff said, after a moment. "I like to think home was the bubble. By coming here, we popped it. Think of everyone we've met. They're all real, out here living their lives. Remember that word the guy at the hostel kept saying, *sonder*? Something about how everyone's lives are as complex as ours."

She laughed and sat up, sipping wine straight from the bottle. "But you're not really thinking about the complexity of their lives, right? You see some random Czech guy and you think 'oh how neat, a Czech guy. I bet he drinks beer and eats dumplings and goulash.' I mean, you could try to get to know him, but you're just a tourist. He doesn't give a shit. He's seen a million of you. Maybe he'll make some small talk, but he lives here. Has to go to work and pay his taxes, all that real-world bullshit. You're never going to see that side of people when you're just some guy who's in town for three days, looking at clock towers and drinking absinthe and shit. It's just a totally different reality. We don't have to live in the real world, not here. I mean, that's kind of the appeal, isn't it?"

"I guess I see what you're getting at," he said, laughing. "It's inauthentic."

"It's not that," she said. "You know what I mean about a bubble? It feels like everyone's out of context. Even the other tourists. Think about who we've talked to, in the hostels. Do you really feel like you know any of them? For instance, look at those people."

Jeff turned his attention to an older couple across the courtyard, who knelt before the grave of Alphonse Mucha. Their backs turned, he could see little more than their grey jackets and fanny packs, both nondescript, signifying very little.

"Maybe the guy's a doctor," she said. "He just retired and this is the trip they've been planning for twenty years.

She's . . . I don't know, a public defender. She's got tons of brutal cases and this is the break she needs. But you don't see that—all you see is a couple of tourists. Out of context."

"I mean, you *could* talk to them. If someone walked up and started talking to us, I think we'd open up pretty easily."

She dipped her head down and picked at some grass growing against the fence. "Guess so. Maybe I don't know what I'm getting at."

"You're getting existential." He put his hand on her thigh. "It makes sense. Nothing but real world for a long time after this."

She shrugged, face falling. "Yeah, that's probably it. Funny how time slowed before the trip. Those last two weeks before we left felt like a year. Now it's almost over."

Sarah turned away to stare at some gravestones, and Jeff's eyes settled on the back of her head, at her ponytail, glowing in the sodium yellow of a nearby streetlight. From behind, she too looked nondescript, and if he ignored the context of their relationship, she could have been anyone, local or tourist. An extra in the background of a scene. Despite knowing better, it left him feeling hollow. He wanted her to turn back around, wanted to see the familiar features of the woman he loved again. Finally, mercifully, she did, and his mind flooded with memories—not just of the trip, but of their lives together.

"Well," he said, leaning in to kiss her cheek. "I'm glad I get to be in a bubble with you."

"That's cheesy as fuck." She smiled anyway, leaning her head into his shoulder. "But yeah, me too."

The clock tower over Vyšehrad rang out seven o'clock slowly, each chime counting down the end of their time together on this trip. He watched her finish her cheese and olives, enamored of the conflicted pleasure in her expression. After the last clang's echo faded, they gathered their things, threw on their bulging backpacks, and followed in the footprints of the tourists gone before them.

] [

While they waited for the bus, Jeff's good feelings faded, replaced instead by a guilt that lay over him like a shroud. He tried to shake it off. Before long, he knew Sarah's existential feelings would manifest in him too.

Who was he kidding? They already had, hadn't they?

They'd spent three long, glorious weeks together; Amsterdam, Berlin, Vienna, Prague . . . it felt like a dream. But they had to wake up some time. Sarah had a job waiting for her back home at a local non-profit—a grants position he didn't fully understand—but he didn't have anywhere to be, not yet. They'd both agreed that he should keep traveling without her, just for a few more weeks. Then, after visiting the Balkans—which had been calling his name for years— he'd return, find a job like hers, and finally they'd settle down into the real world together. Eventually. He wasn't dreading the change, but that didn't mean he was ready for it, either.

They didn't say much on the bus ride to the airport. Sarah's eyes were glued to the windows, her hand to his. They watched together as the bus moved away from the cobblestone fairytale of the city center into far more ordinary-looking suburbs and city streets streaming with cars. The final dredges of day cast sunlight on annoyed-looking men rushing about in business suits, impatient drivers slamming on horns, and homeless people laying in parks nearby. It looked a lot like the real world. Despite this, the walls of the bus still felt like the outer membrane of their bubble, Sarah's touch maintaining the surface tension that kept them inside.

He followed her off the bus when they reached the airport, but there, they had to part ways. He was leaving from the airport's bus terminal, but she had a flight to catch. As the other passengers swarmed around them, Sarah stared into his eyes, as if trying to memorize his face. He returned the gesture. They kissed and hugged and spoke of how excited they were to see each other when he returned home. Just two more weeks.

Finally she could wait no longer and turned to leave, hesitating after taking only a few steps. She mimed a bubble surrounding them, then pulled out an invisible pin.

Pop.

He grinned and watched as she disappeared through the front doors, a glowing warmth trailing behind her that grew colder the further away she walked. In the last few moments she was visible, he watched her ponytail bob and wished badly she would turn around one last time, let him memorize her face again as best he could. No matter how long she stayed, it wouldn't have felt like enough.

He'd expected to be sad at her departure, but this wasn't exactly sadness. He felt alone, unobserved, unimportant. It wasn't unpleasant, just unexpected. The feeling was familiar—one common to life back home, when he was driving to work, or walking his dog, or shopping in a grocery store. Here, though, it felt . . . what had Sarah said?

Out of context. A real world, but not his.

A cool breeze flowed into his sleeves and around his neck, eliciting a quick shiver. For a long moment he stood, watching the people around him. Many were tourists too. Some frantically checked itineraries on their phones. Others strained under the weight of overstuffed bags. A few sat on benches, staring blankly ahead like zombies, waiting for eternity to pass so they could return to their graves. All of it left his gut full of malaise. He felt naked, exposed.

There was time to kill before his bus would leave, but he wished there wasn't.

] [

A night bus had seemed like a good idea. Flights between Prague and Zagreb were pricey, and though he was still traveling from airport to airport, it was far cheaper to take the bus. He'd save on a night at a hostel too, and he could sleep anywhere. Sarah would never have agreed to it, but that was sort of the point. He was alone now. It felt important to indulge in personal whims.

There were only four other passengers. How this could be profitable for the bus company, he had no idea, but he had no reason to question it. His mind so occupied, he paid little attention to his surroundings, barely acknowledging his fellow travelers—they were merely blurs, occupying the other seats. He took up the entire back row, stretching across five spots, and allowed himself to relax. The wine still swimming in his system carried him away, and sleep came quickly.

Some time later, he jolted awake to a blinding light. When he'd boarded, he didn't remember the three overhead lamps being this bright. He sat in the center back seat and looked forward, but none of the other passengers were visible. From outside the bus, night clung to the windows like a thick coating of black paint.

It made no sense for it to be this bright. People took the night bus to sleep, to pass from Point A to Point B with no need to be conscious during the time between. For several moments he sat and looked forward, his position creating a perfect symmetry out of the two rows on either side ahead of him. The seats were all white and perfectly clean, as if this was the bus' maiden voyage.

He reached into his backpack to grab the eyemask that had provided respite in several annoyingly well-lit hostel rooms, but then remembered—they had kept those in Sarah's backpack.

Groggy and annoyed, he stumbled toward the front of the bus, hoping the driver had simply forgotten to shut off the lights. Halfway down, he realized he hadn't seen any of his fellow passengers. Row after row revealed empty chairs. Had they already gotten off? He checked his watch to see how long he'd been asleep, but the symbols on the digital screen made no sense, like an alien language. Maybe the overhead glare was obscuring them. Maybe his brain hadn't quite awakened yet. He tried to calibrate his eyes by looking out the window, but there was still nothing to see. No trees, no stars, not even the road. A perfect shade of black. The effect left him nauseated, dizzy.

At the front of the bus, the driver was almost invisible, only a vague silhouette illuminated by a few symbols glowing on their dashboard. No features. No movement. He couldn't tell so much as their race or gender, even their size.

"Excuse me," he said. "Can you shut the lights off?"

No answer.

"Hello? It's really bright."

Again, only silence. Though the shape of the figure's head didn't change, he sensed it rotate, turn its attention to him, no emotion in the gesture. Jeff stepped backward, hand clammy as he steadied himself on a metal pole.

"Can you hear me?" His voice was faint, riddled with tense vibrations that stuck in his throat. He knew as soon as the words left his tongue there would be no response. Still, he lingered for several moments. The longer he looked at the figure, the less sure he was it was really there. But somebody must have been driving the bus.

Jeff retreated further, looking out the window once again. Were they really moving? An image filled his mind: the bus in a dark void, vibrating every so often to simulate progress. It made him feel as if his eyes were deceiving him, that the world had gone out of focus. Disoriented, he stumbled back to the rear of the bus and laid across the seats again, wishing he had more wine to drown the unpleasant sensations. He curled into a fetal position, closing his eyes and wishing it would all just go away. That he'd wake, and reality would make sense again.

] [

Miraculously, he must have fallen back asleep. That, or he eventually awoke from his nightmare. He opened his eyes to daylight, and the bus was no longer moving.

Jeff got to his feet, eyes heavy with a sleep far deeper than a bus ride should have provided. Images of inky blackness remained lodged in his brain, so he leaned forward to look out the windows, eager to ground himself with sights of a comprehensible world.

Outside had resumed its visible existence. To the left of the bus, a flat, grassy field stretched out for what looked like miles until it transitioned to a forest in the distance. He moved to the right side and was met with the sight of a building no bigger than his former high school, two stories tall and fronted by patches of dying grass. No human activity was visible, nor any movement at all, beyond the light foliage swaying in the breeze.

Jeff blinked a few times, then made his way to the front of the bus. The driver's chair now sat empty, the engine off. Not even an indentation in the seat. He slung his backpack over his shoulder and stepped out onto the dirt.

Whoever had parked the bus seemed to have chosen the spot deliberately. A chain-link fence surrounded the building, but directly before the bus, a metal gate hung open, as if awaiting Jeff's arrival. He slowly walked through it, half-expecting some sort of retaliation for his presence.

Inside the courtyard, he could make out a sign that confirmed he was at least theoretically in the right place. Above the building's main entrance, where chunks of brick lay scattered across the ground, was a sign that read *Zračna Luka*. Below it, the English translation: *Airport*. The words made him freeze in place, examine the building in greater detail. What had remained out of sight from within the bus now confused him all the more. There was no way this was the Zagreb Airport. It looked like nobody had been here in decades.

Across the courtyard, disjointed pieces of architecture jutted haphazardly from the building in different directions. On one side, a long concrete building stretched toward him, connected to the main structure by what looked like still-fresh concrete. The decrepit sign affixed to it read *Bus Depot*. A dozen buses surrounded it, each one stretched long and thin as though it had been thrust into a glass smelter and spun into long, viscous strings.

More disparate structures grew like tumors from beyond the bus depot. Under its steep roof, another sign read *OSTEL*. The crumpled remains of an *H* were piled beneath it. Further still, a sign read *VLAK*. It took a moment for Jeff to recall the Croatian word for train. The sight of one aided him, though it was barely recognizable—one end sat under the steep-roofed station, but the other looked like it had tried to depart while the rear was anchored. It stretched, as if distorted by a black hole, eventually becoming the thickness of a pencil before disappearing in the distance. As it receded, Jeff's mind went with it, recoiling into itself as it failed to interpret these impossibilities. He felt he could not trust his eyes, nor any of his other senses. The effect was dizzying. He doubled over and stared at the ground, hoping that when he looked again, reality would become comprehensible. It did not.

Jeff cupped his hands and called out, "Hello?" but immediately felt his cheeks reddening. His voice didn't echo against the building—instead, it sank into the brick and disappeared. When he stopped to listen, the silence of his surroundings became overwhelming. No birdsong, no wind, no voices to answer.

Never in his life had he craved Sarah's presence more deeply. Never had he craved any human presence at all with such intensity. He swiveled around, breath caught in his throat, looking for somebody, anybody who could make this make sense, but still, there was nobody.

There seemed no choice remaining but to go inside. Jeff hiked his bag up higher onto his shoulder and made his way into the airport. He was greeted by familiar sights. Check-in booths, roped-off queueing lines, kiosks bearing names of familiar airlines. Like the bus, all of it looked new, clean, fresh. None of the decay and ruin that weathered the outside had made it through the front doors. The linoleum floors gleamed with fresh wax, kiosks blinked with welcome messages, conveyor belts moved invisible bags from the lobby onward to the mysterious tunnels that somehow brought them to airplane cargo holds.

He shuddered at the deafening sound of a plane taking off or landing. He nearly sprinted outside to look for it, but the sound grew louder and moved into the airport itself, the great roar echoing through building from ever direction at once. No plane was visible, no matter where he looked. Legs trembling, he weathered the din until it disappeared into the nowhere it had sprung from.

Jeff called out again, and the silence that answered was more oppressive than it had been before. He knelt on the floor, remembering a technique he'd used as a child to escape frequent nightmares. He opened his eyes as wide as he could, spreading the lids apart with his fingers, and focused on the linoleum tiles right before him. But this didn't bring him back to the loft bed of his childhood, nor the soft queen mattress where Sarah lay warm and snoozing beside him. Instead there was only the immaculately clean, cold floor.

An automated voice spoke, making him jump to his feet. First in Croatian, then in English: *"If you don't need to check a bag, please check in at a kiosk."*

He gulped and screamed again and again, lips trembling with a 'b' sound that wouldn't quite come out: *bubble.* Was this the outside or the inside? The thought churned within his mind, spinning his other thoughts into a viscous ooze. He imagined his brain fully liquified, a bubble-wand stuck into it, spreading across a large circle. He blew into it softly and his brain opened outward, detaching and floating far, far away.

Jeff sat back down and lay on the floor, staring upward at white ceiling fans as they turned. His skull felt empty, drained. A minute passed, maybe an hour. The automated voice gave its message several more times. Finally, he got to his feet. He needed to move, to see what else this place contained. Maybe somewhere within, he could find something—better yet, someone—that made sense.

He took several breaths, hoping to ground himself. He summoned his strength and pushed deeper into the airport.

In the next room, he found more endless, clean emptiness. Unmanned security booths, restrooms, waiting areas. All of it silent, waiting for passengers who refused to come.

More automated words in Croatian, then: *"No weapons or liquids in containers over one hundred milliliters allowed in carry-on bags."* Jeff closed his eyes and imagined the many security lines he'd stood in, surrounded by impatient people. In his mind, they checked their watches, shuffled back and forth, muttered annoyances. The longer he left his eyes closed, the more he could hear the bustle around him, feel their presence. He opened his eyes to an empty room, but still he marched his way through the line at a snail's pace, imagining detainments and frustrated protests at petty confiscations.

Once through the imaginary queue, he pushed forward into the rest of the airport, but gate after gate was empty despite lit screens displaying destinations: Sarajevo, Athens, Cairo. Through enormous glass windows, he could see the planes lined up, ready to head to foreign lands, carrying passengers that weren't there.

He kept onward until he reached the airport's final gate. Its destination was displayed in simple letters that put a chill through him:

Stvarni Svijet.

Below it, the English translation: *Real World.*

From somewhere unseen, another plane was landing or taking off, the sounds vibrating the windows as if challenging him to believe it wasn't there.

Then: a flash of movement, past the vacant ticket-checking booth, heading into the tunnel, as if someone were boarding. He dashed toward it. If someone else, anyone, was heading to the real world, maybe he could join them.

Once on the boarding bridge, he saw nothing, noone. His backpack bounced violently on his shoulders as he ran, desperate to confirm he'd seen anything at all. The sunlight from the airport's windows dissipated, leaving him in dimness, and he was forced to open his phone's flashlight feature to light the way. On and on he charged, far further than the bridge should have taken him. Thirty seconds passed, a minute, maybe longer. He began counting the ridges along the sides. Fifty, a hundred, three hundred.

Soon he was panting, legs burning and shaking. No matter how far he went, the plane refused to appear.

Finally, the bridge veered to the left, and he saw the end of a ponytail bounce beyond the corner, barely visible in his phone's dim light. Reinvigorated, he resumed his mad dash. Another corner, another glimpse. He embraced his delirium and cried out her name, chasing the echoes in vain.

What felt like hours later, he took a final turn and saw the conclusion of the boarding bridge. It did not end at a plane's open door, but instead at a plain wall, and there she stood. He could barely see her with his meager light, but he would know that ponytail anywhere. Panting and wheezing, he staggered toward her.

"Sarah," he said, softly at first, then louder, when she did not respond.

When he was close enough to touch her, he reached out and put a hand to her shoulder, but his fingers slipped through the shadows of her form. He tried again, but she was incorporeal, an ambivalent ghost.

He longed for her to turn around, a desire like hunger or thirst.

"Please," he said, breath huffing. "Please. Turn around."

When she refused, he pushed past her, dropping his bag and putting his back to the wall she was facing. But even from this direction, he couldn't see her face. The ponytail extended from the front of her head too, from every direction at once.

The flashlight flickered, and his phone buzzed with a warning: *Low Battery*. How long ago had he turned it on?

She stepped through the wall, exiting his view entirely. Jeff fell to his knees and covered his eyes, weeping. When he finally opened them, he was in total darkness. He clicked his phone, but it was dead, and all light gone with it.

portal

S.E. DENTON

I hadn't talked to Zack in over a year. The last time was when I dropped him off at Turquoise Harbor Recovery Center after his third coke bust. I said something like, "You got this."

Less than three months later, I read in the papers that he'd gotten another DUI. The industry press and entertainment magazines feasted on it, as always. Somehow his lawyer got him off pretty clean, meaning no jail time.

Zack went into hiding after that. As he explained to me on the phone, he'd sold off everything—his house, cars, boat—and got some small place up near Laurel Canyon, away from everyone. He was sober, he said. Starting over. But he honestly sounded worse than ever.

I need your help, Dylan. Please. You're the sanest person I know.

Which was sad, because I was a mess in my own way. Two divorces. Barely making ends meet with all the alimony and no real gigs anymore. People recognized me wherever I went— mostly middle-aged women—but for a life that was so long ago, it was hard to believe I was even the same person. I wasn't. But between Zack and myself, I was the stable one. Somehow my mistakes had never ended up in a Hollywood tabloid, while Zack had become the poster child for what Hollywood can do to a child actor. I remember reading once about Cronus, the god of time, in a book on mythology. He ate his own children and vomited them back up.

That, in my opinion, is Hollywood.

] [

I drove up Laurel Canyon, thinking about how things actually turn out so differently than what you expect. 1986 to 1990 treated us very well. We were teen heartthrobs. It started with a dumb, kiddie Halloween adventure flick called *The Secret of the Ghoul Prince*. That's when I first met Zack. Fourteen years old. Both of us felt a bit embarrassed about being the stars of a children's movie, but shit it was fun. And it made us a lot of money and set us both up for the rest of the 80s. *Beach Bums. The Heartbreak Twins. Summertime Drag.* Millions of dollars. When I turned sixteen, I bought a Ferrari. What fucking sixteen year old actually needs a Ferrari? I had access to whatever I wanted. Booze, drugs, women. I was sleeping with four girls on average every weekend, some at the same time. And not all of them were girls. A lot were women who knew better. It was sick, honestly. All of it. But at the time, it felt like perfection.

Zack's place was a small, old bungalow-style house perched on a tree-infested slope and nestled back against a hill, with a flight of flagstone stairs weaving up to the rustic house. It was a relic, left over from a different era of Los Angeles, and the complete antithesis of Zack's former Malibu home. The white paint was peeling and the shingles were a weathered gray. The whole place seemed shrouded in a fog, except for one thing: the bungalow had a red door.

Oddly, that's what disturbed me the most: that red door.

Zack must have heard my car, because before I even unfastened my seatbelt, the red door was wide open and there he was, standing on the edge of the porch, looking down at me. Even from a distance, he looked as bad as he'd sounded on the phone. His once-golden hair had long since faded into a grungy shade, now bristly and greasy. He was a skeleton in a blue tank-top and basketball shorts, grinning at me, his arms hugging his bony body.

As I got out of my car and started up the steps, a terrible feeling ballooned in my stomach. I wanted to throw out a cheerful hello, but my throat closed and instead, I said nothing.

I made it to the top of the stairs and came face-to-face with that disturbing grin. It struck me then that everything about Zack had become concave: he was folding in on himself. His bloodshot eyes were pulling everything in, like black holes. He was slowly imploding. Drugs. Clearly drugs. Although he'd insisted on the phone that he was sober, I'd learned to stop believing him a decade ago.

He hugged me like a child who hadn't seen their father in months.

"Hey, Z," I said.

"You look good," he told me.

"Thanks."

"You working out?"

"Some," I said.

Zack smelled terrible. He stood there in the doorway, grinning and nodding, his arms folded across his caved-in chest. It was like he was guarding the place, keeping me outside.

"We gonna go in?" I asked him.

"Nah, nah," he said, and gestured for me to follow him around to the side of the house. There was a flagstone patio with a small table and chairs that looked out into the trees. On the table was a sweaty pitcher of lemonade, literally the last thing I'd ever expected Zack to ingest.

I took a seat and watched Zack attempt to settle in the chair across from me, but he couldn't sit still.

"Lemonade?" he asked.

"Sure."

"I got hooked on it when I gave up drinking and everything," he told me, picking up the pitcher. "Plus it's so goddamn hot here."

Despite the shade, it was sweltering. It was the humidity. Like a jungle.

I watched him pour two glasses of ice-laden lemonade, sloshing some of it on the table, his hands unsteady. His face and neck were drenched in sweat. I'd witnessed him do a lot of things that were unsettling over the years, but nothing was ever so goddamn excruciating as watching Zack attempt to pour two glasses of lemonade without it ending in disaster.

"Thanks," I told him when he put down the pitcher and handed one of the glasses to me.

His hands were shaking so bad, the ice cubes clinked. I took a sip and waited patiently. Zack chugged half of his lemonade, then spit an ice cube back out into the glass.

"So . . . what's up?" I asked him.

"Well . . . there's no way I'm gonna be able to say any of this without sounding crazy . . . and I guess maybe that's a real *possibility*. That I've officially gone crazy."

"Okay," I said.

"So I'm just going to tell you . . ."

I waited.

His fingers laced and unlaced. His leg jittered beneath the table. He seemed on the verge of combustion..

"Just tell me, Zack," I said. "Come on."

"Okay, so . . . well, I've been living in this house for only, like, a month, right?"

"Nice spot," I told him.

"It seems that way, doesn't it?"

"But it's not?"

"I think there's something going on here," Zack said.

"Okay."

"At least I think so."

"Like what?"

"I'm just going to show you."

He stood up. I took another sip of lemonade, then set down my glass and stood to follow him. He led me through a side door that opened into a small, shadowy living room with beamed ceilings. The air was thick, stifling. Other than a couch, coffee table, and a flat-screen TV hanging on the wall, the room was empty. There was a pillow and a blanket on the couch, and the coffee table was littered with a full ashtray, empty glasses and soda cans, dirty dishes. I noticed a framed movie poster from one of our 80s hits leaning against one of the walls. Zack and I posed on the railing of a Santa Monica Beach lifeguard stand, shirtless, wearing sunglasses and wise-ass smirks. *Beach Bums.* All of my framed posters were in a storage unit in North Hollywood, hidden far away from my daily life. Zack and I had always been different like that. He clung maniacally to the things I struggled to forget.

Just then, Zack stopped at the beginning of a hallway, and flicked on a light switch.

"There," he said, pointing at something at the end of the long hallway, except there was nothing. There was a door off to the side at the very end that led to the bedroom, and another door only a few feet away from where we stood that looked like a closet. The carpet was an old, disgusting brown, the walls a nicotine-stained white.

"What is it?" I asked.

"Do you, like, see or maybe . . . *sense* anything, at the end, over there?" Zack said.

He held himself tightly again. There were goosebumps on his bare forearms.

I stared at the end of the hallway and felt my skin start to prickle. A sense of dread swelled in the pit of my stomach, and I was suddenly very scared.

"I don't know," I told him. "I definitely don't *see* anything . . ."

I kept my eyes focused on the end of the hallway, the hairs on the back of my neck stiffening. I realized then that

I was waiting for someone—or something—to walk out of the bedroom. But that made no logical sense. We were the only ones there.

"Just tell me what's going on," I told Zack. "I don't understand."

"Let's go back outside," Zack said.

We went back out onto the patio, into the heat. The icy sensation on the back of my neck gradually melted away, but my sense of dread did not.

"So," Zack began. "I was sleeping in the bedroom the first week or so when I first moved in, but I couldn't sleep. I mean, I'm under a lot of stress, and feeling all sorts of anxiety about everything, and being sober. So, I'm just not sleeping well in general. But I was having these intense feelings of terror in bed. And I kept thinking that someone was in the house. I'd get up and check the locks and everything. I mean, this place is small, so if it was a person, I'd know if someone was inside with me. But the feeling wouldn't go away, and I thought maybe if I tried to pinpoint where the sensation was coming from, I could get to the bottom of it. At first, obviously, I thought it was coming from inside me. But it wasn't. Sure, there's all sorts of shit going on in my head and body, but I'm not the origin. At least, I don't think so."

I nodded, but not because I agreed.

"And then, one night, I was staring at the spot just directly on the other side of the bedroom door . . . the spot at the end of the hallway. And at that moment, it became very *clear* to me that the reason I was feeling so scared and terrified was because of that particular spot . . ."

I nodded again. I didn't know what else to do.

"I started sleeping on the couch. I can't even use the bathroom in the bedroom anymore. I've been going outside . . ." he said, pointing to a part of the overgrown side yard, "Over there."

This explained his atrocious body odor.

"It's gross, I know, but I can't go anywhere near that hallway," Zack said. "Something very bad is there."

"But . . .what?" I asked.

"Well, I've done some research," he said. "I think it's a portal."

"A . . . portal?"

"Yeah. Like a doorway."

"To what?"

"To another plane. You know, a door that spirits use."

"Like . . . fucking *Poltergeist*?"

Zack nodded, very affirmatively. "I know, it's crazy," he said. "Trust me. I feel crazy. I'm even willing to accept that I *am* crazy, .but I need you to determine that for me. You know me, man. You *know* me. I need you to stay here with me for a few days and come to your own conclusion. I trust your opinion."

"Wait, you want me to stay here? With you?"

"Yeah."

"To see if there's a portal in your house."

"Precisely."

I leaned back in the patio chair, put my hands over my face, and rubbed my eyelids. I listened to the sound of the birds and the wind in the trees. A mosquito buzzed near my ear. When I opened my eyes, I saw red. A bead of bright crimson snaking out of Zack's right nostril.

"Dude," I said. "You have a nosebleed."

As soon as the words left my lips, it was like a faucet inside Zack's head turned on. Blood began gushing out of Zack's nose, cascading over his lips and chin and splattering on the front of his blue tank top. I lurched up, out of my chair, looking for something to stop the blood. He took off his shirt, wadded it up, and tilted his head back to stanch the flow, but within seconds, the shirt was saturated.

I couldn't understand how so much blood could come out of one person's skull.

He started to cry. It was terrifying, seeing this person I'd known practically my whole life, hemorrhaging blood, tears, and fear.

"Dylan, man, I need you," he screamed, his hand grasping my shirt. "I *need* you here."

"Okay, Z," I said, grabbing his shoulder, hoping that would steady him. "Okay. I'll stay for a couple of days, all right?"

"Thank you," Zack said, his grip loosening. "Thank you."

] [

The nosebleed was obviously a product of his chronic battle with cocaine, but the timing disturbed me. Maybe moments of severe stress can bring about abrupt nosebleeds, but all of it creeped me out. After we got his nosebleed under control, I told him that I was going back to my place to pack a bag and deal with some phone calls, but I'd be back.

"Before dark," he urged.

I made it back to his place with about an hour of daylight remaining. Zack had ordered a pizza, but neither of us really ate much of it. We reminisced a bit. He blended up some type of weird non-alcoholic margaritas made of Sprite and lime juice, and we watched *Beach Bums*—something we initially thought would be fun, but by the time the credits rolled, my mood was muddy.

"Think I'll hit the hay," I told Zack.

He finished off his fourth or fifth glass of fake margarita and stood.

"I'm going to go sit outside for a little while," he told me.

Fresh sheets were folded and set out on a chair that was blocking the door to the bedroom. I picked them up and carried them with me, trying to be aware of how my body felt as I neared the area of the so-called portal, but I was too tired to feel much of anything.

I made up the bed, took a quick shower, and brushed my teeth. The sheets were somewhat cool as I slipped between them. I avoided looking at the spot out in the hallway as I turned off the bedside lamp. The hallway light was on, so I eventually shifted my gaze over to the door, to the spot. The pizza and fake margaritas were starting to give me indigestion, and the ceiling fan directly above me made an obnoxious clattering sound.

For the longest time, I lay there, wondering if I'd sleep at all.

] [

When I woke in the middle of the night, sweating, the sheets were tangled around my body, but the room was freezing beneath the churning fan. I sat up.

Something was very *wrong*.

The shadows were thick in all directions.

I turned my head toward the hallway. Stared into the dark there. I swore something moved. A *shift* in the shadows. Again, that sense of dread swelled inside of me.

I blinked several times. Gradually, my eyes adjusted to the dark.

No more shifting shadows.

I watched the spot for several minutes and then lay back down.

At some point, I fell back asleep.

] [

The next morning, the fear I'd experienced during the night felt remote, then absurd. A nightmare was the most logical explanation. Even when I stepped out into the hall and felt a chill right in that precise spot, I convinced myself that I imagined it.

There was a pot of coffee in the kitchen, and Zack had left out a chipped red mug for me. I poured a cup and went out to the patio. He was there, smoking a cigarette, fixated on something high up in one of the trees.

"Morning," I said.

"Yeah." He pointed upward, toward a series of short, abrupt chirps. "Hooded oriole."

I glanced upwards just in time to see a blur of flaming orange fly away.

"Since when are you an ornithologist?" I asked him.

"A what?"

"How did you know what type of bird that was?"

"I bought a book about birds and read it," he said. "Learned about the birds in L.A."

A simple explanation, but mind-boggling. Zack could barely function in daily life and yet he'd found time at some point to study and memorize bird species. What else was inside of his skull? If beaten and broken open enough, Zack was a piñata, full of strange surprises.

"Well," Zack said. "How did you sleep?"

My mind replayed segments of my nightmare, although it hadn't been a true nightmare. More like a rerun of my own real-life memories, but reenacted within the syrupy landscape of dreams. I chose not to say anything *specific* about that. Instead I told him, "I did wake up in the middle of the night feeling a little uneasy, but I think it was because of a nightmare."

"What was the nightmare about?"

I took a sip out of the red mug. "Can't remember."

The hooded oriole flew back and landed on a nearby branch. It fluttered its wings and shat onto the patio. The disgusting white splatter distracted Zack enough that he didn't interrogate me further about the night.

"Do you want to go get some breakfast?" he asked. "Get out of the house?"

"Sounds great."

] [

Neither of us had an appetite.

We sat in a booth at Mel's Diner poking at plates of fried eggs, hash browns, and sausage with our forks and taking the occasional bite. Zack had ordered a side of pancakes that remained untouched, bathing in a pool of butter and syrup, growing mushier by the second. Maybe it was all the caffeine in my system, but it felt as if things could fall apart if I so much as *breathed* too deeply. And when the crumbling happened, a terrifying alternate dimension that had been lurking at the peripheries of our realities our whole lives would finally be revealed.

"I just don't understand how . . ." Zack said, stabbing his fork into one of his fried eggs. A river of golden yolk bled onto the plate, onto his hash browns. "How . . ."

"How what?"

"Well, how you went to the same parties and did the same drugs as me, and you didn't . . . you didn't turn out like I did."

I hadn't anticipated this sort of conversation. All along I'd been thinking about the cold spot at the end of the hallway. I'd thought we were on the brink of a very unsettling conversation about *that*. Oddly, a conversation about addiction was just as disturbing. I suddenly craved a cigarette, and I hadn't smoked in twelve years. Things were too intense. I stuffed a piece of cold toast in my mouth, then immediately regretted the decision.

"I just don't understand what is wrong with me," Zack said.

I couldn't answer right away. I had to chew the toast. Force it down my throat. It gave me time to think about how I wanted to reply.

"Look, Zack, some people are just more susceptible," I told him. "Biologically, you know."

"Right. I know," he said, staring at the tiny jukebox. "It's a disease."

"We aren't different," I told him. "Nothing is wrong with you."

Although, we *were* different. And I was pretty sure there was something wrong with him.

But as I watched him take a bite of soggy pancakes, those thoughts didn't extinguish what I felt for him. I've always had friends. But I've never shared the sort of bond Zack and I have with any other person, and I probably never will. I loved him despite all the heartbreak he'd put me through as a friend; despite whatever heartbreak lay ahead. There was an urgency for me to step in and stop the next catastrophic accident from happening. I had never really done so, even though there were a dozen opportunities in our past to help, but it always felt too big for me to handle. However, I could do so now.

Or at least, I could try.

] [

Darkness poured into my eyes like ink. I couldn't see a single thing. I felt the slickness of sweat all over my neck, back, and face. Chilled deep down to my center despite the electrifying blaze of panic coursing through me. My body was in a state of complete paralysis. I couldn't even breathe. All I could do was stare into the darkness.

My eyes gradually adjusted, and I could detect a form at the end of the bed. Blacker than the darkness around it. Shifting, ever so slightly. Looming there at the end of the mattress, so close it could reach out and grab my feet. I didn't know what that thing could possibly be, but the energy it gave off was soul-curdling. There was nothing blacker, nothing darker than that *thing*.

It moved.

I watched in dumb horror as the shadow-thing glided through the darkness. My neck wouldn't budge, but my eyes followed it as it moved toward the door. It reached the boundaries of my vision—and then it was gone. Something in the air, in the darkness, shifted. Suddenly, I was aware of my body again, beyond my pounding heart. I could feel my fingers. My toes. I reached out and fumbled with the lamp on the bedside table. Light. My eyelids closed tightly and twitched. My eyes were overwhelmed by the sudden opposite of utter blackness.

When I felt able, I opened my eyes again and looked over toward the door, at the place at the end of the hallway. I know beyond a doubt that the thing went there. Disappeared into the space there. It had visited me in the night, but I had the very distinct feeling that it hadn't been looking for me.

It was looking for Zack.

It could have done terrible acts to me; that is without question. But it didn't. I wasn't open. I wasn't another door it could slip through or a room it could occupy.

It could not nest in me.

] [

While I was about to recount what I'd experienced to Zack the next morning, my agent, Richard, called. It was a relief, because the encounter I'd had was something I didn't want to share out loud. If I didn't share it, it could very easily be written off as a horrifying bout of sleep paralysis, which could perfectly and scientifically describe what I'd experienced the night before. If I did share it, though . . . there was something about speaking it out loud that made the incident feel *unscientific.* Supernatural, even.

"Richie, hey," I said, into the phone.

"Dylan, good to hear your voice. Great news for you."

"What's that?"

"*Law and Order: SVU.*"

"What about it?"

"One of the guest roles came down with some kind of pancreatic thing. They need a replacement immediately. Like, tonight."

"Tonight?"

"Yes," Riche said. "As in, get your ass to an airport in the next few hours and fly to New York."

"Like, *now?*" I said.

"You got it."

"Is it worth it?"

"Worth it?" Richie said. "Dylan, you haven't had a role in over ten months. Of course, it's worth it. Goddamn."

"You're right. Okay. I'll fly out here in a few."

"I already have it arranged," Richie said. "Just get to LAX by 11:40. United Airlines."

Everything was suddenly moving so fast and felt so shockingly bright.

"Okay," I said. "Hey, what's the role?"

"You're a predatorial pharmacist."

"Superb."

"Call me when you get to the airport. I'll fill you in with the rest of the details."

"Sure."

When I hung up and looked at Zack, I saw that his face had turned pale and doughy.

"You have to leave?" he asked, his voice dry.

"Yeah, man, I'm sorry. It's the first break I've gotten in months. I have to take it. As soon as I'm back in L.A., I'll come here," I reassured him. "If you need me, just call."

Zack sucked in a quick breath and nodded. He had the eyes of a feverish ten-year-old who's just been informed that the long, menacing needle in the doctor's hand was going to be inserted directly into their spine.

I'll never forget that look.

"I'll only be gone a day or two," I told him. "You'll be okay, Z."

"Yeah, I know."

Of course, I didn't believe it.

But I left him anyway.

] [

Traveling to New York (and the all-night shoot that followed) was so hectic that I forgot all about Zack—and the hallway—almost entirely. It wasn't until housekeeping woke me the next morning that I realized: he hadn't called. Believing that was a good sign, I texted Zack to check in, then took a shower, packed, and headed back to the airport.

He did not text me back. I called him before I boarded the plane, but there was still no answer. I called him again just before takeoff, and then put my phone in airplane mode, worry and guilt gnawing at me.

Most likely, I told myself, Zack was mad at me for leaving and was ignoring me; he had never been the emotionally mature type. He'd once refused to talk to me for three weeks when we were seventeen because I wouldn't let him ride my new motorcycle.

When I landed at LAX, I texted him that I was on my way over.

I called him when I was standing in front of his house.

He wasn't on the patio. He didn't answer the front door.

] [

The only trace of Zack was a trail of dribbled blood leading from the living room, terminating at the end of the hallway. I explained to the police that Zack got really bad nosebleeds, but even I felt unconvinced. They had a blood splatter expert agree, but the investigation into Zack's disappearance dragged on for months. In the end, there was no evidence that any sort of crime had happened, so it was dropped. But the internet and tabloids continued to have fun publishing theories, most of them outrageous.

For me, however, reality was way stranger than any fiction written about Zack's disappearance. I had absolutely no answers. The blood trail leading to that *spot* haunted me. Why would he go toward the portal or whatever it was? He was afraid of it. He wouldn't, would he? What if the blood trail wasn't from a nosebleed? Then what was the cause of the blood?

There was no one I could talk to, no one I could tell about the portal. I couldn't tell the police about what I'd experienced those two nights I slept in Zack's room. I did my own research. Read things on the internet about portals and shadow people, which was the closest thing I could find to describing what I'd seen at the end of Zack's bed. I thought about calling up this one paranormal expert in California, but halfway through dialing, I felt embarrassed and stopped myself.

The house sold quickly, once the police ended their investigation, then went back on the market months later. Another person bought it. Put it on the market eight weeks later. I thought about reaching out to the former owners to find out why they'd sold the home—had they seen something, too? But, in the end, I didn't contact anyone.

Deep down, I knew what happened.

That space at the end of the hallway, that invisible hole, was responsible. Sometimes I convince myself that it had been waiting for Zack his entire life. Maybe it was the only place he was ever destined to end up. The blackness that had nibbled on him from within since his youth finally swallowed him whole when no one was looking. Turned him into a feast for the shadows.

No Hollywood ending here. Just another soul devoured.

] [

The months following Zack's vanishing did not go well for me. Jobs weren't coming in for TV dramas or movie roles, my usual sources of mediocre paychecks. I could only score spots as a celebrity guest on dumb competitive reality shows like *Celebrity Bake-Off*, *Celebrity Undercover Boss*, and a pilot for a ridiculous show called *Star Wars* about two celebrity teams going head-to-head in epic laser tag battles. Additionally, that fall, one of my kids started high school and the other started middle school, and they both found me suddenly embarrassing, probably sharing the perspective of my ex-wife. I didn't know where my life was going, if anywhere.

It was the middle of the week, and I experienced an unexpected bubble of motivation amidst my depression, and started to clean my apartment before the optimism burst. I was dragging the laundry basket out of the closet, over to the chair in the corner of my bedroom, flinging clothes into the basket—and that's when I noticed it. The same cold, prickly sense of dread, unfurling deep inside me—the same terror I'd felt when staring at the end of Zack's hallway.

My fingers went limp. I dropped the crumpled shirt in my hand to the floor, stumbled backwards, and plopped onto the bed, not taking my eyes off the chair, off the entire corner. No question. Something was very wrong over *there*.

During good times, when I kept things tidy, the chair looked cozy, accessorized by a floor lamp and a throw pillow. However, I never actually sat in it. I never had a reason to sit in the chair when I had a sofa in the living room. It was purely aesthetic, the whole set-up. If it weren't for the clothes mounting over the course of two weeks, I might have gone on not noticing. But from that moment on, it became impossible not to sense the *wrongness* of the corner.

That night, I couldn't fall asleep. I wouldn't allow myself to leave a light on. I am older now, and have no valid excuse for a nightlight, beyond the icy, tingling knot in my gut, which I keep telling myself is clearly some branch of anxiety, split off from my current bout of depression; some latent trauma, tied to leaving Zack alone in his house while I flew to New York.

If only I hadn't gone. If I'd just gotten him out of there.

In the corner, behind the chair, a shadow begins to move. My breath lodges in my throat, my whole body from my neck down to my toes, frozen. I watch the darkness shift upward, as if something is peering out from behind the chair, studying me. The only thing I can do is blink. I blink several times and focus again.

Nothing. Trick of the eyes.

I complete my breath and take another. My body loosens slightly, enough to reach out and turn on the bedside lamp. In the light, there is nothing but my own mess.

I'll take care of all that tomorrow. Maybe move the chair to the living room.

I lay there for hours, keeping my eyes on the corner. Thinking of Zack.

#blessed

ANGELA SYLVAINE

Cecilia, better known as **@ccseeme**, stepped from the car, adjusting the Yayoi Kusama pumpkin print scarf at her neck, the perfect pop of color against her fitted white blouse. She pursed her lips very slightly and cocked one hip, knowing how spectacular she would look with the industrial warehouses as a backdrop. Her sponsors would love it.

But no cameras flashed, and no voices called out, demanding to hear how she'd managed to secure tickets to [F O L L O W], the mysterious new pop-up art installation. She didn't know either, not really. The tickets appeared in her email inbox like any other exclusive event or party invitation. Unlike the others, not a single person she knew, besides herself, had received this invite. While everyone was talking about the exhibit, no one had seen it. No one even knew where it was, and she'd been warned that sharing the address would result in denial of entrance.

Cecelia had assumed they'd have some media lined up, though, or what was the point? She glanced at her phone, thinking it couldn't hurt to text that guy from TMZ to capture a couple pics of her on the way out, but she had no signal. Strange.

The car they sent for her pulled away, leaving Cecilia alone on the deserted sidewalk. She was running a little late, well, a lot late. Everyone else was probably already inside the squat, windowless, cinderblock structure. She entered, the glass doors labeled [F O L L O W] opening with a whoosh, splitting the word in two.

A black hallway extended before her, ending in a swell of blue light. The clack of her heels filling the space, she approached an archway surrounded by cool, blue neon. She stepped through to another hallway, this one white down to the opaque glass floor. Still not a single person in sight.

A black metal rack with four rows of protruding rods held a single, hanging museum audio guide on a strap which bore her name woven in gold thread.

"Cute," she said, and her voice echoed around her, repeating, softening, disappearing.

If she couldn't get professional pictures, she'd take her own. Her followers loved candids. She removed the device from the rack, hooked it around her wrist, and raised it to her ear. Using her free hand, she raised her phone for a selfie. Neon halo, head tilted, lips bowed in a slight smile, button clicked.

The picture came back a wash of static, and she frowned. Must be something about the neon.

"No photos," a mechanical voice said from the speaker, though she hadn't pressed any button. There was no echo this time.

She surveyed the space, searching the corners for the telltale half-globe of a camera, but nothing marred the pristine white surface. Really, what was the point in being there if she couldn't show anyone? Cecelia didn't even like art, didn't get it, especially the modern stuff.

"Gaze or Go, now," the voice said.

A ding sounded behind her, from the direction of the front door, and she looked back to find a sign flashing GO in neon green.

She scoffed, the sound reverberating, warping, pitching up into a giggle. A chill shook her shoulders, but she told herself it was just the AC.

"Gaze or Go. Now," the voice repeated.

The word **GAZE** appeared on the floor in front of her in brilliant white block letters that seared themselves into her gaze, preceding another set of glass doors marked [F O L L O W].

"Or Go," the voice said, rising higher, becoming that giggle. Mocking her.

The doors swished open, revealing only complete blackness beyond. She clenched her teeth and strode forward, already thinking of what she'd tell her followers, how she'd destroy this ridiculous installation online.

As soon as Cecelia crossed the plane of the doors, the sound of her footsteps stopped though she continued. White spots from the blazing vibrance of the hallway still spotted her vision, unreal orbs floating in the darkness. Her own inhale and exhale rose around her, the air panting faster and faster, not stopping when she held her breath.

The spots faded and her vision cleared, revealing only total darkness. She raised the audio guide, the red light at the top her only illumination.

Blinking into the dark, she swung the device before her like a torch, and glimpsed a shape just a few feet away. Another person. Startled, she gasped and took a step back. "Hello?"

Her voice didn't come from her throat, but from the speaker. She gaped at the thing. How were they doing this? She looked back at that person, just standing there, not moving.

"Hey, you!" she yelled, again from the speaker.

"Shhhhhhhhh." The admonishment rose, surrounded her, pressing against her lips, wedging its way into her mouth.

Shaking her head to free herself from the veil of sound, she turned, ready to barrel toward the brilliant light beyond the doors, but there were no doors anymore, only darkness. Her eyes had begun to adjust, and she saw more shapes, more people. Not moving. Standing perfectly still.

"Who's there?" she whispered, but didn't, the device hissing her voice.

She spun in a circle, sure the exit had to be there, that she'd just gotten turned around. But there was no door, no light. Only the shapes, the people, circling her but barely visible by the minute red light of the speaker.

"*#fashion*," someone said, close by.

She whirled, now face to face with a woman. Same height, same hair, same scarf.

Herself. Mouth pursed, hip cocked, head thrown back. Ready for that photo against the backdrop of warehouses.

Cecilia stumbled backward, thumping into another body, another person. Another her, this one clad in her Versace kimono robe, with eyes closed and face raised to the sky. "*#blessed*," the woman said, though her mouth didn't move in her frozen face.

"This isn't funny," she tried to say, but the device in her hand giggled, that same mocking sound.

She shoved past the blessed woman, out of the circle surrounding her. But there were more, and she stumbled into another Cecilia. This one's mouth stretched wide, too wide, exaggerated smile showing tongue and teeth. "*#beautiful*," this one said, but she wasn't at all.

That's not me, Cecelia wanted to shout, but she swallowed down the words, couldn't hear her pleas funneled through the tainting crackle of the speaker.

She plunged further into the darkness, hands extended, bumping into bodies that stood like mannequins but weren't, had soft skin and muscle that gave beneath her grasping fingers. Dozens of them, all her, with expressions frozen in exaggeration. She shoved past, knew if she could just reach a wall, she'd be able to follow it to the door.

"*#scared*," the one nearest her said, skin stretched taught across sharp cheekbones and eyes bulging and glassy, ready to pop.

Cecelia shrank back. Don't touch that one, she thought, and pressed her lips together tight but couldn't stop the whimper that escaped the device. It grew and spread until all of the versions of her whimpered. The sound swelled to a deafening pitch then disappeared, as if eaten by the void.

The wall had to be close, the room couldn't go on forever. She flailed her arms, thumping into bodies that wavered but didn't fall, rooted in place.

The Cecilias began to discolor, each successive one fading, skin and clothes tarnishing, turning sepia. Each one a photo she'd snapped and filtered and uploaded and shared. She bit her tongue to keep from crying out, swallowed her own coppery blood as she pushed farther, deeper.

She kept going, kept shoving through the throng. The hers paled even more, all color seeping away, draining to a stark noir. "*#nofilter*," one said, and she grabbed its hand, raised in a peace sign.

"Please. What is this?" she begged, her voice dangling at her side. The fingers she clutched bent like putty and polished nails slipped free from oozing, gray nail beds.

Cecilia shrieked from the speaker, couldn't hold back as her own nails fell into the darkness. She collapsed to her knees on the cold, black floor, tearing at the strap, but it had cut through skin and muscle, burrowing into her wrist to become a part of her.

"Let me out of here!" she screamed, dragging her plastic voice to scrape along the ground as she crawled through the legs of the hers. Legs that led to feet riveted to the floor with giant nails driven through skin and bone, and Christian Louboutins.

But no blood, these hers didn't bleed. Body trembling, she forced herself to keep going, cringing every time she brushed up against one of them. Sobs shook her shoulders and hot tears leaked down her cheeks. My mascara, she thought.

A bright light flashed, drenching the room, singeing her eyes.

She caught a glimpse of another room, of not-hers. Other people. It went dark again but she crawled in that direction, uncaring of the throbbing pain in her knees.

Her head thumped hard into glass. Finally, a way out. She stood, pounding the surface with her palms, the speaker emitting her frantic screams as it thumped against the barrier.

The light flashed again, and she froze. A group of people she didn't know, didn't recognize, stood on the other side of the glass, some looking at her, some at the room behind her, with interest. Others talking or distracted on their phones.

Darkness again, total, no hint of light.

Cecelia screamed again but this time the speaker only crackled and said, "*#influencer.*"

From the other side of the glass, they laughed.

the lights

JOSEPH ANDRE THOMAS

I turned onto the overgrown side road, trees on either side running spindly, wooden fingers across my car windows. My headlights illuminated a moss-covered sign announcing Fallview Hospital three miles down the road; a loud orange construction notice had been affixed below it: *Abandoned Site—Do Not Enter.* The sign had blackened and frayed at the edges. I was a little over three hours from the nearest city. This road felt like a vestige of another dimension.

I'd been tipped off to this derelict hospital by one of my followers. My first thought upon learning about it: How on earth did I not know about this place?

My second, more powerful, thought was: This is going to make *killer* content.

My beat-up old Audi crawled slowly over the cracked pavement, the serpentine road ahead wending into the darkness. The foliage had grown so wild the road was thin as a driveway. The last thing I needed was a branch right through my windshield. It was a balmy evening, a bit windy but warm—ideal for a ghost hunt. A bright gibbous moon strobed above me through the limbs of the trees.

After about ten minutes, I reached a sight familiar from my internet research: the Fallview Hospital entrance. Like the road, it was in the throes of returning to nature. Vines clung tightly to the hospital's brick exterior. Roots burst up through the cement of the parking lot. One tree, alongside the building, had grown right up through a window on the top floor. The sign above the shattered glass doors read:

F llview Hosp t l.

"My god." I stepped out of my car and said, to no one: "It's perfect."

Nearly tripping over some busted granite, I rounded my car and popped the trunk. I removed my GoPro, strapping it around my head, and my sport-pole for selfie diaries. Bare-bones filming equipment for sure, but since I was going solo—and had no idea what condition Fallview's interior was in—I wanted to travel light. I slung my backpack and sleeping bag over my shoulder.

My phone had no bars—dammit. Not a surprise, filming out in the sticks, but I'd passed a small township a few miles back, so I'd held out hope that I'd have some data for a livestream or two. Getting live time on Instagram added to the effect (the "verisimilitude," as Jake, my pretentious editor, liked to say). It also cut down on haters spamming *hoax* and *fake* in the comments. My channel, Ghost-Hunter-Kelsey, was healthy for its size—43k followers, good engagement, C+ Social Blade rating and rising—but it was a far cry from the biggest ghost-hunting accounts.

Oh well—I'd get as much raw footage on the GoPro as possible and a handful of diaries. Jake could cobble five or six quality posts from that. I attached my phone to the sport-pole, framed the front of the ruined entrance behind me, and hit record.

"Hey guys, here at Fallview Hospital, an abandoned medical facility." I angled the selfie to fully take in the shattered front doors. "As you can see, this place is an absolute *wreck*. Post-apocalyptic, practically. Fallview opened in 1922 and went out of operation in the mid-90s. Apparently some real estate mogul purchased the land, but never did anything with it, for some reason. In the early-aughts, in that post-*Blair Witch* horror scene, some filmmakers shot a found footage movie here, but it never got released. That's about all I could find online." I checked my watch as I marched up to the front door. "It's 10:30 pm now. I'm going to head in, look around, and, as always, spend the night. Join me, won't you?"

I turned the camera off, thinking once more about retooling that catchphrase. When I started using it, I'd been going for a creepy/catchy refrain, *à la* "You've just crossed over into . . . the Twilight Zone!" or "Submitted for the approval of the Midnight Society . . ." But it just didn't have the same *oomph*. It also ran the risk, as Jake pointed out, of someone taking it literally and actually trying to join me. I got enough creepy DMs and requests to start an OnlyFans without giving terminally-online weirdos encouragement.

My heart fluttered as I approached the two-storey ruin. You'd think that after spending dozens of nights in abandoned buildings like this one, my anxiety would have waned. But there was always fresh danger—danger that had nothing to do with ghosts. Could the ceiling collapse? Could it be home to rattlesnakes? Rabid wolverines? Ne'er-do-wells, holed up after a bank heist?

I stepped through the broken glass into the foyer, scanning my flashlight over the reception area: white walls, rows of white chairs, a long, S-shaped desk stretching from one end of the room to the other, also white, and partitioned into various sections with big hand-painted, red-letter signs: Intake, Visitation, Consultation. There were two hallway exits, one to the west marked Hospital, the other,

Processing, stretching east. Several long light fixtures ran the length of the ceiling, their bulbs, surprisingly, still intact. I vaulted over the Consultation desk, scrambled over some overturned filing cabinets, and found a lightswitch. I flicked it on—nothing.

Shocker.

The Hospital wing beckoned me, but the doors were shut. Just as I went to remove my trusty bolt cutters from my backpack, I spotted, on the floor, a rusted, crumpled chain. It had been cut cleanly in two places, long enough ago that even the sliced sections had begun to rust. Local hooligans or fellow ghost hunters, probably; either way, I appreciated the assist.

I entered a hallway lined with broken windows, a few with branches poking through from the overgrown wilderness outside. Intact light fixtures, again, ran along the ceiling. I whipped out my phone and EMF meter, recording a little update—naturally adding a few embellishments on the many 'clear signs' of supernatural activity I'd noted so far.

The hall was long and twisting, and my flashlight hardly made a dent in the darkness. I'd tried to find a floorplan of Fallview online—no joy—but this wasn't my first abandoned hospital. They may appear labyrinthine, but most generally follow a pattern. You won't get lost if you know what you're navigating.

One thing that did set this hospital apart from others were the lights. It was odd to see a building this long-abandoned in which the lighting remained in such good shape. Bulbs were usually either removed before the building was vacated, or shattered over time, as a result of exposure to the elements. These looked new, practically untouched.

I entered the Labs/Imaging wing, an open, arterial space leading to dozens of rooms and offices populated by some furniture, the odd bit of mouldering machinery, more empty file cabinets. It struck me, however, as I peered into what had once been an ultrasound room, that it wasn't just the light fixtures; *everything* here was in good shape. There was the usual loamy smell—rotten wood, I guessed; black mold, undoubtedly—and anything of value had been long ago picked over, but what remained was relatively organized and clean. And white, so very white; the original milk-and-eggshell aesthetic was apparent even in the dark. As far as abandoned facilities went, this was pretty pristine.

I had an odd thought, then, and jogged back to the entrance. It took a moment to find the building directory. I noted a room labelled *Electrical*, down the Processing hall, opposite the first one I'd entered. I navigated another hallway, a mirror-image of the first. It didn't take long to find. The electrical room was a ten-by-ten mess of power boxes and wiring (all of which looked to be mostly intact). I found what I thought was the main breaker and turned it on with a rusty *clunk*.

The darkness persisted.

Of course. It had been a shot in the dark—literally—but stranger things have happened. Given the state of everything in here, it had crossed my mind that perhaps this place was in the midst of being renovated, with an eye toward reopening. Or perhaps to make it more appealing to a prospective buyer. A ghost-hunting girl can dream.

I spent the next two hours wandering the hallways: the surgical wing, personnel offices, pediatrics. They were in largely the same condition as the other spaces. There wasn't much to the place, honestly. It was creepy, in the way that all abandoned spaces are, but not *frightening*. The wind and forest ambiance were audible, but there hadn't even been an unexpected noise I could play for a jump scare. I recorded a few more diaries, trying to summon up worry at my surroundings, but my heart wasn't in it.

Eventually, I started yawning. I found the patient bedrooms and took the first one, across from the visitor check-in desk. The bed didn't have a mattress, but I found a few fusty old bedrolls stuffed into a hall closet. I set one up and recorded a final diary, as I always did, tucked into my sleeping bag. I really emphasized the "feeling" of this place, my "concern" about spending the night here, wondering whether "the spirits" would take kindly to my presence.

Once finished, I muted my phone, popped a melatonin, and lay down. It isn't like I *don't* believe in ghosts. It's just that I've never seen anything to convince me, beyond a shadow of doubt, of their existence. If anything, I was more of a believer *before* I started this channel. As a girl, I'd sensed things around the house—entities, presences, whatever-you-call-em; I was *sure* that ghosts were real. As an adult, though, nothing I'd seen had ever codified those beliefs. Didn't matter what equipment I used. EMF readers, night vision goggles, thermographic cameras—all that, just to see what I could have seen with my own two eyes. Not much.

My channel, though, is no cynical grift. I don't think. I can't deny that I leaned into it once I started seeing strong social engagement, with the catchphrase and the all-nighter shtick, but I *wanted* to be convinced, truly wanted to sense those things I'd sensed as a girl. Had it really just been my overactive, childish imagination? I somehow didn't buy that, either.

Maybe that's what this whole endeavour was truly about. Despite the evidence—or lack thereof—a part of me still believed.

] [

When I awoke, I don't know how much later, I opened my eyes to blindingly bright light. With a yelp of shock—an almost physically painful sense of surprise—I immediately shut my eyes again. It was as if someone was shining an industrial-sized flashlight directly in my face.

"The fuck!?"

I rose slowly, blinking rapidly, trying to adjust my vision to the enveloping white light. I had to shade my eyes and squint just to see, such was the incandescence pouring through the hallways and bouncing off the white walls.

"Hello?" I called out. "Is someone here?"

I walked back into the hallway, barely able to open my eyes. All the lights seemed to have come on while I was asleep. I guess I'd simply found an inoperative electrical room? The grid of this building was clearly working just fine.

These lights, though . . . they were *shockingly* bright, especially radiating against the white walls. Hospitals are, of course, usually well-lit, but this was brighter than any hospital I'd seen before, as if the lights had been somehow supercharged. My eyes couldn't even adjust, I could only keep them open for a few seconds at a time. It was as difficult to navigate the brightness as it had been the complete darkness.

I spotted a set of switches behind the visitor's desk. I flicked the first. Nothing changed. Waggled the second, third, fourth. The lights continued to beam. Were they connected to a different power source? Some sort of strange security system?

"Hey guys, this is absolutely *eerie*," I said, after packing up my sleeping bag and backpack. "It's ten past three. I woke up and it's like *all* the hospital lights went on at the same time. This is insane. My heart is beating like a drum right now. I feel like you guys might even be able to hear it." I held the phone to my collarbone, above my heart, for nervous comic effect. "I don't know, but it gets even weirder, check this out." Still filming, I flipped my camera and moved back to the light switch. I recorded myself trying them all again. "I'm no electrician, but I've never heard of a building having lights like this before. Some kind of emergency backup? If any of y'all know what's going on here, hit me in the comments."

I hadn't needed to force the enthusiasm that time around. My blood pressure was firing. Finally—something truly weird!

Strapping the GoPro on, I searched through the patient bedrooms—all white, all clean. Then I made my way back down the hallway toward the reception area. It, too, was fully lit, brilliance spilling through the broken front windows and onto the hood of my Audi. I returned down the second hall, back to the imaging wing. All lit up.

As I walked, I filmed everything. GoPro. iPhone. Shaky-cam. Verité-style. I'm usually much more careful framing and blocking my diaries, but I wanted to capture my sense of frenzy. (There's your "verisimilitude," Jake.) Didn't much matter anyway; as far as I could see on my iPhone screen, I was consistently backdropped by a flat, luminous white.

By the time I reached what had been the administrative offices, I was convinced: Every single light in the entire building had come on. It must've been a security system. But why these lights, not an alarm? Unless a silent alarm *had* gone off, and some private security company had been alerted. I chuckled at that. Who would bother retaining security on a place like this?

I made my way back down the east hallway and returned to Electrical. There were several breakers. The biggest one loomed directly across from the door, presumably the main power source. I pulled the handle down, but the lights remained on. I tried the two other breakers, flicked them on and off. The lights didn't even flicker. I triple-checked that each breaker was in the off position. I got multiple shots of each breaker being turned on and off, over and over again.

Incredulous, I backed out of the electrical closet. Just what the hell was going on in this hospital? Could there be another electrical room, in the basement maybe? This had been the only one marked in the directory. What would be the point of a building having two? That also didn't explain why none of the switches worked.

Back in the welcome area, I recorded one final diary. I stood in front of reception and recounted my final walk through the hospital. Jake could intercut it with the GoPro shots of me trying different breakers. There was a tremor in my voice as I signed off the diary. One I wasn't faking.

After packing up my stuff, I had a thought, and approached one of the desk lamps on the reception desk. Like all the other lights, it beamed brightly. What was the wattage on these bulbs? I followed its cord to a wall socket and yanked out the plug.

The light kept shining.

"What the fuck?"

The lamp taunted me with its steadfast glow. It didn't flicker, fade, dim. Impossible, I thought. I placed my phone at an angle on the desk, filming myself as I reached out to touch the bulb. It was *hot*—white hot—I could tell, even from inches away. I'm not sure why I persisted, but I did, pressing the tip of my pointer finger against the bulb.

"Fuck!" I recoiled immediately, my fingerprint burning.

I stared at the lightbulb. My fingertip pulsed with hot pain. Bulbs get hot, of course, but *that* hot? It was like lava. One second longer on that bulb, and I'd have had a third-degree burn.

Suddenly, I startled at a waft of cold on the back of my neck—*freezing* cold, a stark contrast to my scalding finger. I looked behind me, around me. There was nothing there but stark, endless white.

"Christ, Kelsey," I muttered. "Now you're jumping at the wind."

I pocketed my phone, stepped out the front doors, and got into my car. To hell with this place.

] [

I pulled off the highway into the township I'd passed on my way out here. There was a roadside motel with—thank god—a 24-hour receptionist. It was past four in the morning, and I was too exhausted, mentally more than physically, to make the drive back to town. It didn't help that Fallview seemed to have burnt my retinas. I'd had to squint just to see through the windshield, rubbing my eyes every few seconds. The road seemed a hazy mishmash of warped lines and haloed streetlights.

I paid on credit card and walked up to the room the stoned receptionist assigned me. The hallways were dead quiet, their soft yellow lights a stark contrast to the shocking brilliance of Fallview. I collapsed in the musty motel bed immediately and might have knocked off, but thought better of it.

Now that I had WiFi, my followers would be expecting something.

I posted the first diary I'd made—the one at the entrance, before going inside the hospital—and the first one I'd recorded after waking up to all the lights on. I had *way* more footage than that, but I figured those two would be a good teaser.

After posting both, I silenced my phone and lay back down. Despite my exhaustion, my mind kept running. Even without reviewing it, I could tell I'd gotten great stuff. I'd talk to Jake, get him to whip up some effective reels. Maybe I could convince him to come back with me. Maybe one of the bigger ghost channels would even be interested in a collaboration. If that went well, we could create something longer, a twenty or thirty minute doc. My Instagram presence was fine, but I *had* been meaning to step up my YouTube footprint.

I laughed to myself—*at* myself—as I lay in the bed, realizing that, as soon as I woke up, one of my followers, an electrician probably, would condescendingly teach me something. (They loved any excuse to be condescending.) It had just been a haywire emergency system. The desk lamps probably had batteries in them, so they wouldn't burn out in a crisis situation. That bulb had been red-hot due to, I don't know, prolonged inactivity.

There'll be a rational explanation, I thought, as I shut my eyes. There always is.

] · [

I awoke with a start to a loud noise, instinctively kicking the sheets off the bed in shock. Knocking at my motel door.

"H—hello?"

"Wake up call, dude." A sleepy male voice floated through the door. "Checkout at eleven."

I blinked a few times, his footsteps receding down the hallway. The bedside clock read: *10:33 am*. I rose, back aching. You couldn't just call? Damn, man. I pulled my jeans on, hands shaking as though over-caffeinated. Jittery from the rude awakening, from the night before.

Had that all really happened? Even just a few hours later, it felt like a distant dream. Scanning the motel room, the lazy ceiling fan and cheap flatscreen and tiny table with Lego-sized coffee maker, I couldn't tell if the colors were always this dull and muted, or if exposing my pupils to last night's near-nuclear levels of brightness had permanently washed out my vision.

I started preparing to leave, checked my phone. Stopped dead in my tracks.

Seventy-six notifications.

I opened Instagram. I'd received several *thousand* hearts on the second video already and there were hundreds of comments—wow! I scrolled through my DMs, looking at a long list of messages from names I didn't recognize.

Tidus&Yuna4ever: "Yo wtf is that."

Cronibaba: "What's that behind you?"

pastramiboy42: "r u alive? pls babe"

candelabras-n-cocaine: "WOW, that is one of the scariest videos I've ever seen. Did you . . ."

JimboDaHimbo: "Uh what????"

a_sad_of_sandwichs: "I don't care if u faked that, its one of the CREEPIEST things i've ever . . ."

DiscoStuAdvertisements: "Who is behind you?"

I noticed a message from a username I did recognize: *Jake@StarlightEditing*. "Yo Kelsey, did you go out and film with someone last night? You should have told me. Are those prosthetics? How much footage did you get?"

Prosthetics? What on earth?

I tapped back to my main Instagram feedback and clicked on the videos. Nothing immediately stood out as odd; everything was just as I remembered. But one word kept popping up in the comments.

Behind.

Behind.

Behind.

I sat back down on the bed and opened the original second video file, the one after the lights had come on. I hit play, and zoomed into the background behind as the image of me spoke into the phone camera. Nothing seemed amiss at first.

Then I saw it.

There was a shape behind me, pressed up against the wall. An irregularity. I must have glanced past it the previous night, because I'd missed entirely when I uploaded the clip. It was as white as its surroundings, and might have seemed like nothing, just a quirk in the architecture of the hospital, if only for . . .

The eyes. The grin.

My nerve endings shuddered as I reopened the clip in my video-editing app. I viewed the negative, then cranked the contrast.

Nearly threw up.

Behind me stood a man—extremely tall and thin and naked, his skin sheet-white, his back pressed up against the hallway wall. His eyes were fixed on the back of my head, leering; his mouth a fishhook smile. He was bald, except for tufts of sweaty gray hair sweeping the sides of his head. He stood so still, I might have mistaken it for a photograph, if it weren't for me yammering on in the foreground.

When I opened the other videos I'd taken last night, I nearly dropped my phone. There were six video diaries where the iPhone camera caught the background behind me. I watched one after the other, closely; each took me a moment to find him, but there he was: freakishly tall, well over six feet, perhaps even seven. His skin was so colorless, so pallid, that he was camouflaged against the walls. He was as difficult to see in that flooding white luminosity as he would have been in the pitch dark.

In each clip, he followed about twenty feet behind me, sometimes pressed against the wall, sometimes hunched behind counters and desks. In most clips, he was stock still; in others, whenever I turned a corner or glanced behind me, he moved—*fast*—breaking that statuesque composure, scuttling on all fours across doorways and behind cover. The phone mic didn't pick up so much as a single patter of his bare feet. Whenever he repositioned himself, he'd go instantly still again, slowly reorienting himself to stare—to *leer*—at me.

And maybe it was my imagination, but once in a while his eyes flitted from the image of me on-screen, to me right now—looking directly into the camera.

In the final clip I'd recorded—the one where I touched the desk lamp—he moved directly behind me, closer than he had in any other clip. He clamped a hand over his mouth. He seemed to be holding in laughter. I'd been too preoccupied by the lights to notice.

Just as my finger came into contact with the hot lightbulb, the tall man peered over my shoulder, that awful grin just inches behind my head. When I pulled my hand back, he had to stop himself from laughing again.

Then, while I stared in shock at the bulb, he leaned in even closer. He *breathed* on the back of my neck. Before I'd even had time to turn around, he was gone—melted back into the lights.

I sat there, on the edge of the motel bed, for I don't know how long, scrubbing the videos backwards and forwards, backwards and forwards, my mind unable to process the hideous sights on the little screen, until another sharp wooden rap on the door nearly stopped my heart.

"Eleven," said the motel employee. "Hard out!"

Dazed, I grabbed my bags and splashed water across my face. My mind moved as though through a fog, lurching and limping, yet somehow as vacant as a condemned building.

As I left the room, I hit the lightswitch.

The lights did not go off.

Stomach lurching, I turned to the ceiling fan light. It remained alight. So did the bathroom and bedside lights—mocking, teasing. I backed up against the door, palms sweating. I scanned the room, every corner, for hidden eyes.

The lights gave one final, powerfully bright flare, and then—as I ran out of the room—extinguished.

"Demon!" It Shrieked

KEN HUELER

My wrists are duct-taped behind a chair, my ankles zip-tied together, my pockets emptied. The burlap hood is wrenched off, tearing out scalp hairs. That pain pricks the start of tears. I blink them away: a counter with cabinets—like in a doctor's office—bare, except for a powerful yellow-and-black lantern flashlight aimed at the ceiling; blank, blue-green walls; and a clock, hour hand at nine and minute hand at twelve.

The man circles from behind and lowers his face to mine. He's more square-headed than I remember, and this time his full, brown hair is slicked back. The light bouncing off the ceiling blacks out his eye sockets; the shadows trickle down his hawkish nose and into his mouth. He smiles; the left canine is freshly missing.

"Almost seems real," he brays, gesturing at the unfurnished room. When he tilts his chin to smirk at the clock, brown eyes surface on his face; eyelids flutter like gasps. The hawk nose swings back to me. "Soak up all you want for a description, reporter, but you can't see my face. Not really. We have blind spots, see, where the optic nerves emerge on our retinas. Right now, mister, for you, part of my face does not exist. But your brain fills in the missing part, just like it does for bits of roads when we drive, or when we read lying words in the center of your lying sentences. Not. Really. There."

I've prepared for this. Journalists have to, especially those of us fighting junk science and conspiracies. But over the years, complacency lulled me into thinking this would never happen to me. Now that I'm here, though, actually here, it feels unreal, impossible.

Dust and insect corpses coat the floor, I hear no sounds outside, and he felt no need for a gag—we're somewhere abandoned, isolated, and this time no one will drag him away. My sweat burns and freezes at the same time.

I am not prepared.

To control my panic, I keep memorizing: medium build, aging blue jeans with whitening wrinkles, blank clover-green t-shirt with a fraying collar, yin/yang tattoo on the left forearm, thick scar top of the right wrist...

He backs away. "Why quiet now, and not before, when you were spewing all those lies? If you'd just let people clear their minds, we could see the exit and leave."

Keep him talking. "Exit to where?"

"To reality." I flinch as he slaps his palm against an armrest. "We only know what our brains can perceive. Everything is in our heads. Our heads, see? If you let us change how we think, we could tear through the illusion, find the way out. But people like you want to confuse us, anchor us here."

To my left is an open door and, across a dark corridor, the ghost of another room. The man didn't fix me to this chair, but I can't run with bound ankles. "I'm just a journalist with a background in science. I fact-check and explain. I never speculate about the unreal." I tense my wrists. The duct tape gives, but not much.

He smiles. "Exactly. The Illuminati formed to combat superstition and religion. Science to rule us all! To keep us here and docile, more like it. Weaponized facts. But your truths are based on a dream world. And you repeat your misinformation so often that people believe it." He leans against the counter. "So hard not to."

I force my voice steady. "I'm not keeping you anywhere. I'm just a regular guy, like you. Got a son back in Indiana. Maybe like beer a little too much." Pushing back despair, I spread my heels and get a glimmer of hope: My ankles aren't bound as tightly as my wrists.

"How does liking beer humanize you? Yes, losing a father is terrible, terrible, but as you know, journalist, it happens all the time. A world where anything, no matter how horrible, is possible, shouldn't be real. I don't want to orphan your son, but to open the exit there must be a sacrifice, and it must be willing."

Leverage his logic, his rules. "I am not willing."

"Oh, I'll get you there, just like you persuade the naïve to inject children with autism and dull the truths of visionaries with antipsychotics." He steps behind me, tests the binding on my wrists. "I need out, and that liminal gap between the past and the future, or those gaping holes made by our optic nerves, might allow that. I just need the background noise to stop, so I can concentrate." I tense when he rests his hands on my shoulders. "But you, see, you're like a dangling tree root on a cliff," he curls his fingers into my muscles, as if he's about to strip them off my back, "keeping me afraid of letting go. But close my eyes, cut the root, I'll land back in reality, not die. Stop making me afraid," he yells. "You can't terrify me anymore, hear?"

"You kidnapped a journalist." I can't keep the tremor out of my voice. What will he do behind me, where I can't see it coming? "You won't escape to anywhere but a prison. Add bodily harm or murder, you'll never leave. Cut me loose. We can work this out."

He relaxes, lets go, and comes back to face me. "But killing someone in a dream is not a crime. Deeds are bad, thoughts are not, and you are just my thought in this, my dream, or, maybe, in yours." He turns to the counter, swears. "With all that planning, of all the things to forget." He grabs the flashlight. "I'll be back. You know sight lies; what happens when we take it away?" He swings the beam into my face, flooding my retinas before I can shut my lids. The world swims with colors and shapes. I hear his footsteps turn outside the door. To the left, I think.

Alone, blind, the fear I've been tamping bursts like a swollen appendix. It almost overwhelms me, but I force it down—no time. I breathe. Focus. Of course I've researched what to do: I've gotten death threats. I slip off my shoes and lift one leg. The socks help slide the zip-tie down, but it scrapes like hell. I shake my other leg free, stand, and then step backward over my bound arms to bring them up front. The man will be back, maybe in seconds; I'll deal with the duct tape later. I hurry toward tiny slivers of light in a room across the corridor, but at the doorframe, I stop.

I've left my shoes.

I physically anticipate the man barreling out a doorway, or turning a corner, or brushing fingers across my face in the dark. Guts squirming, I flee right, toward a brighter, more promising glow. The corridor opens onto an atrium, and I can see again! The moon's out, somewhere, but not visible in the skylight. Windows are boarded—the slivers I saw earlier must be gaps between plywood and window frames—as are sliding glass double doors, but an unprotected, half-oval window above them gives me hope. I tear around the atrium, peer into rooms, but there's nothing to stack, just dust and blue-green walls.

The silence is impossibly solid. Either my captor's not back or he's quiet in his disappointment. The second floor has more light—maybe its windows aren't sealed. Hurrying to the closest of the atrium's matching stairs, I notice a directory: This was a hospital. Alabama has a ton of closed rural hospitals.

Upstairs, the landing opens on each side to door-lined corridors, but directly ahead, in a bare lounge, are broken windows. I avoid the scatter of stones and glass shards— almost. A sting in my right sole stops me dead. I work the sliver out and keep going, but slower now.

Outside, I see a parking lot, a boarded-up restaurant, and, miles away over broad woods, a powdery smear of light that must be a town. The moon is still low. A lot of night ahead to be without a flashlight.

I lean out, to locate fire escapes. They're disconnected and spread across the grassy strip below like toothy, dislocated jaws, along with twisted bike racks, and upright metal garbage cans that would section me like cookie cutters. The trees have been sawn slantwise, into vicious canine stumps. Jumping is not an option.

I've been avoiding the sill's broken glass, but now I lower my wrists over a large shard and begin sawing at the duct tape. Thread by thread it separates—and then the glass snaps. Pain startles awake just below my thumb; blood pours, and I shove my hand against my chest. The shard cracks against metal below, announcing my location. I need to move. I lift my arms high, then swing them down, hard, pulling my wrists apart as I do. The duct tape rips the rest of the way. I should have done that first off.

Back at the landing, I'm deciding which corridor to try when I hear charging footsteps downstairs. I freeze. Running might give me away. Something is tapping the linoleum by my feet. Blood. I pull off one sock and wad it against my cut.

The man is in the atrium, shining a flashlight across the sealed double doors. His other hand holds a knife, a large one. With that flashlight, he can get around faster than I can. I don't move, don't breathe.

He swings the beam up to me. Light and shadow transform his pale cheeks and widows-peak forehead into a grinning mask. "Where will you go? For both of us there is only one way out, and it is not through this door behind me.

While I have you, heretic, tell me: Why is there is no Grand Unification Theory? Fact-check your universe, journalist. How do you reconcile two conflicting sets of physics? And is the universe made of vibrating strings? Holograms? All your theories are shifting and fantastical and dense. But a dream, a dream explains everything."

"We learn through trial and error," I shout, glancing both directions. I need to find an exit he missed. Someone so carless—or crazy or both—who forgets their weapon, who doesn't secure their victim properly or lock the door, has to have missed something. Get outside. Disappear into the woods.

He takes one step toward the stairs nearest me and stops. "What do you really know, journalist? History is written by the winners, but losers have stories too, and often more true." He laughs. "What happens here will be defined by who gets out."

He runs, not up the stairs but back the into the corridor we both came from. Why? I'm unarmed and so close. I rush down the corridor on the opposite side of the building from him.

Or is this the direction he expected me to go? It's so predictable.

The doors all hang open. Beside them, darker blue-green rectangles with creamy white scribbles show where number plates have been torn off. Rooms on the left are dark; the ones on the right offer a stingy moonlit glow.

Clacking. Claws on linoleum. A dog? I back up. If he put a dog—or dogs—up here, what are they trained to do?

An animal, large and low to the floor, emerges from a dark doorway, and two reflecting, polished eyes swing toward me. It's a raccoon. After what feels like minutes, it waddles through the nearest right-hand doorway.

I feel a wave of relief. Then I realize: Birds can fly through broken windows, but a large mammal means something climbable: a tree, or a still-attached fire escape. I peer into the room the raccoon appeared from. I can't see in the windowless murk, but, right fingers trailing the wall,

I explore. Nothing but a second door, which is shut. The raccoon didn't entering the building here.

I run across the corridor, following the raccoon's path. This room is moonlight, a reception counter, and, to my right, a clock frozen at 3 o'clock above the only other door, which is open. That leads to another office, as empty as the last. Across from me is a door whose clock died at 12:15, and more open doors to my left and right. I go left, into a large empty room with no other exits and lots of windows, most of them broken. Moonlight bouncing off fallen glass shards projects a mosaic—white, broken birds in flight—onto one wall.

Nothing outside the windows is climbable, and below are more wrenched bike racks and dead fire escapes. I turn, breathe, exhale. Blind wandering will get me nowhere. I need information. As I think, I stare above the door, at a clock set to midnight, but the only ticking is an angry pulse from my cut, reminding me of the time I don't have.

The building's layout. Figure that out first.

Back in the previous office, I turn left and find myself in a small hallway. Right would take me back to the corridor, I think, and forward is another wooden door, but left is a pair of closed, swinging double doors. Through those is a large room, probably for staff meetings or presentations, with many windows whose broken glass refracts jagged white shapes onto the wall—a woman dancing. That image, projected from a flat surface, triggers a memory.

] [

"What about the Holographic Universe theory?" the disheveled man had asked—same blue shirt, but no missing tooth.

I'm in the Q&A section of my presentation, the last hurdle before beer and ribbing with colleagues. "What about it?"

Both his hands clutch the microphone tighter. "If that's true, see, our universe is a 3-D projection off a two-dimensional surface. Everything that we see," he swings the microphone, "is an illusion. That's science."

"Then I suppose the Flat-Earthers were right," I answer. After the chuckles die down, I smile. "Unless proven, it's just a thought experiment. Yes, ma'am, you have a question?"

The man shields the microphone. "Write an article about how the universe is a dream and changes every time we look away."

The woman tries to coax the microphone away from him.

"Little, almost unnoticed changes," the man continues. "Do animals really adapt to their environment, or do you say that to disguise that we don't remember them right?" He screams, high and frantic, at the insistent woman, then turns back to me. "Why are you keeping us here, where nothing is real? At least tell us why."

There is a scuffle, shouting. Security intervenes.

] [

In the next room I enter, a dark circle on one faded wall matches size with a nearby clock over the door opposite me. I stare. The rooms have all been empty: no posters or calendars or trashcans—not even a paperclip. Everything taken away. Except clocks. I look above me. The door I came through has a clock. A door on the right, probably leading back into the corridor, also has one. Why would one room need three clocks? I examine each. I can't see dust on two of them, but that clock near the wall circle has thick, obvious dust striped by recent fingers.

Even crazy people have a logic. If I can understand how he thinks, I can outsmart him. I ease the blood-soaked sock from my thumb. The blood is slowing. I toss the sock into a corner, peel the other off, and press the cleaner part to the cut. I look up at the repositioned clock's face: The hands are at 9:45.

As I turn to check the other clock's time, a shadow darts across a trapezoid of moonlight on the floor. 'Rat!' I think, jumping away. But I heard nothing, hear nothing.

No, something flew past outside, most likely a nighthawk or a bat. I study the floor, panic: To make that trajectory, whatever it was had to be flying straight up. Birds and bats dive to snatch prey, but none launch straight up.

I suck long breaths to slow my heart. I'm wrong. Of course I'm wrong. Light takes time to reach our eyes, and time to reach our brain, and the brain takes time to process. For us to navigate this always lagging world, our brain applies physics, geometry, and experience to what we saw last and offers a probable future for when we arrive in the present. Everything seen happened already and, like the missing middle of that man's face, is a guess. My emotions just overloaded my brain, that's all; I remember it wrong because anxiety screws with short-term memory.

The next room has four doors and four clocks—two, above me and opposite, are at 12:30; the other pair is at 3:15. The left door is a dead end, the right an empty closet, and the forward one leads to a room with more doors and clocks.

The clock hands! Do they indicate throughways? Or is my desperation forcing a pattern?

I test my theory in the next three rooms. The hands are indeed guides. I can move quickly if needed and not get cornered. I continue searching, more confident now, until I realize I'm passing up doors I 'know' go nowhere. But any one of them could hide something useful. I wanted inside the man's head, but I can picture how he might have hacked into mine: knowing my analytical mindset, he sets up the clocks, assumes I crack the pattern, and waits until I stumble into his lap. I check all the doors.

A scream—not fear, but anguish, and muffled: It has to slink around corners to reach me, from far enough that I'm safe for now, but if he breaks down, my chances to negotiate vanish.

I glance outside. I thought hours had passed, but the moon still hangs low. Without a working clock, time is subjective.

No.

The moon is lower, setting. Because of that first clock, I saw what I was expecting, a rising moon—confirmation bias—but the clocks are all dead. How many wrong assumptions have I made?

"A dream makes sense while you're inside it," the man yells, closer now. "People like you keep the dream going, but we'd wake if you'd let it run off the rails."

I assess my chances: I can avoid being trapped, but picking around broken glass barefoot will slow me, and he knows the maze. I need to find out where he is. I hurry to the main corridor, crouch in a doorway two rooms from the landing.

"You're a logical man building a logical dream," the man roars, "but knowing how I see your creation would break you."

Bare walls scatter his words. The man is mounting the opposite atrium stairs one step at a time, as if he's exhausted. "Time slows down and speeds up. You know it does, journalist. How do we know whether we sleep nine hours or forty-five years?" He crests the stairs. The flashlight washes everything in its path, but behind it, the man is dark: His blue jeans appear black, his shirt a Stygian blue. He sweeps the beam, stops, and aims it at the floor. Light bounces back at him and . . . his shirt is green. That's right, it's clover green. Why did I remember it blue? Because memories degrade—that's why journalists interview people as soon as possible.

The man moves my direction, eyes down, and drops to all fours. The knife—it looks bigger—clacks on the tile. The flashlight illuminates his face like a painted saint's as he examines the blood droplets from my cut, and then his tongue spills out and writhes fatly, like a salted slug, across the tiles. He snorts, then follows the trail toward the broken windows until the wall corner hides him.

I'm about retreat back into the warren of offices and exam rooms when he jumps into the corridor, startling me frozen.

"The game is almost over," he bellows. "Let me out!" He storms across the landing, to the opposite corridor. The crack and clatter of scattering plastic echoes as he swings his flashlight against the wall. He turns gray in the moonlight, and then black charging through a doorway.

If I keep moving, I'll run into him; if I stay in one place, he'll find me. What should I do? I work the bloody sock loose. I'm no longer bleeding. I'm about to toss my sock when it hits me: With him up here, in the other corridor's rooms, I can collect my shoes. And then explore the direction he headed to retrieve his knife—hopefully from his car.

I creep downstairs. As I cross the atrium, I hear, then see, something drop from above, bounce on the floor, and skitter as echoey, tick-tacking fragments. I stare up at the landing, but no one is there. A bit of broken flashlight, balancing on the edge, must have slipped off, that's all. I'm almost to the corridor when I realize: Light travels faster than sound, but when the plastic dropped—and when the man smashed the flashlight—I heard before I saw. I was close to both incidents. Up to a certain distance, our brains edit sight and sound so we experience them simultaneously. Like when adding blind-spot noses to faces, our brains change reality to help us.

But mine isn't.

No, I'm panicking. That changes perception.

Slow footsteps above enter the landing. "Dreamers are easier to control," the man shouts. "Why do the words 'demons' and 'dreamers' sound so alike? Because, demon, the two are one."

I press against the wall, not moving. Against this wide white paint I'm ridiculously obvious, but he may not look down. The corridor is so close, so sheltering, but human peripheral vision excels at picking up movement, and I can't slip into that darkness, not knowing where it leads, with him following.

Wait—aren't all the hospital's walls blue-green? No, just on the second floor.

He stops and addresses the empty corridor: "Religion is your partner," he roars. "Hell to make us afraid of letting go; Heaven to keep us in line. You use those fears to stop us from questioning, and then invent science to make this world seem real." He laughs, and lumbers into the rooms I explored.

He doesn't know I'm down here!

I re-enter the corridor, feel my way back down the wall. One doorway. Two. After nine I hit the end, a locked crashbar door. I start back. Which door did I escape from? I judge the faint atrium glow, unable to remember how distant it had looked. I know—or think I do—I didn't come this far, but it wasn't the first few doors. I enter a middle door. No chair, no shoes. I stumble back out and into the next room. On the wall I see a faint glow, the luminous hands of that first clock, still reading nine o'clock. I fumble until I find the chair and feel around for on my shoes. As I tie the laces— delicately to not reopen the wound—I realize: Not enough light would seep through the boarded-up window for the hands to glow. The man moved the clock from outside, and he did so today. A person that meticulous doesn't forget a knife. He wanted me to escape and run the maze. He wanted to make me doubt, to change my mind, to destroy my ability to reason. The blood-licking was a performance. He knew I was watching.

And he knows I'm down here.

I exit the room and dash toward the atrium's glow. The man is nowhere to be seen. I run upstairs and check both corridors. He emerges from the raccoon door and shuffles, eyes on the floor, into the one across from it. I slip into the other corridor, into the first moonlit doorway. I want as much distance as possible, but we'll run into one another eventually. I run to a window. Dawn can't be more than an hour away. He knows I'm searching for exits, thinks I'll keep trying, but what if I hide in a closet and wait out the dawn— once I can see, he loses an advantage.

But which closet? Not one this close to a corridor. While searching for the perfect shut door, I'm confronted by the only clock so far with a second hand, a red needle pointing right, to a door whose clock has no face, just a rim, a square plastic movement box, and hands stretching up to midnight. This outlier, with its extra hand, is at 9 o'clock, like the one glowing downstairs. Is that clock from the first room the solution to the maze? Does the right-hand door lead to an exit? Or a key? Or will it be empty, a cruel joke? Knowing I might be playing his game, I turn the handle.

The man charges out, his impossibly dilated eyes so close to my face that our breaths roll into each other's lungs. I stumble backwards, and my mind falters: The middle of his face—that hawk nose—is missing, just gone, and my brain won't stop licking at that ragged empty circle like it's a stringy, sour hole from a freshly torn-out tooth.

I had prepared myself for flight—learning the building's layout, reclaiming my shoes for speed—but that all dies, leaving me helpless, floating in shock, waiting in slowed time for when that raised knife plunges.

And I realize this *is* a dream, and this *is* an exit, but it's not my exit—it belongs to this monster.

"Dreamer!" it shrieks.

where we are, where we were, where we will always be
Erik McHatton

We are being driven by a car made of meat down a road composed of squashed marigolds and the eyes of rabbits. The buildings around us are rubberized, metallicized, or melting into pools of ice cream. A man runs by, his face twisted into a silent wail, skin bubbling with the faces of a thousand plastic babies. There are people fused to the sidewalk, their bodies slowly turning to concrete. Others struggle and flail while sinking slowly into puddles of black morass. The smell of warm licorice fills the car, briefly casting out the stench of rotten, burning pork that wafts in from the vehicle's fleshy engine.

I shudder to think what it's using for gas.

The puppet still dominates the sky. Clara says it remains the same for her; same black suit, same wooden limbs and painted-on face. To me, it looks like one of those fuzzy, sleevey things that psychiatrists use to get little kids to show them where their uncle touched them.

Clara's moving further away, becoming more presence than person. The longer this goes on, the more unreal she feels, even though she's sitting right there, squishing up out of the seat, craning her head out the window to get a better look at the puppet to see if it's still there. It is. She's sitting there doing that, but she might as well be inside a painting, or in a television show. Like everything else, she's becoming chimerical, as foreign as the tiny orcas raining from the sky and spattering against the windshield, or the slimy mucus that seeps out of the steering wheel moving itself inside my hands.

I'm not sure where the car is taking us, or if we'll even be in the same car when we get there. Maybe, by that time, it won't be Clara next to me. Maybe it'll be you. I'm not sure how this works. Why can you hear me, see me? Are you the one doing this? If you aren't, then for your sake I hope you don't end up here. I hope, for your sake, you stay right where you are. I have this feeling that as long as you're there, I'm safe.

But if you were here . . .

] [

I was the first to notice. Clara and I had gone to some dirtbag motel off the interstate to celebrate one of those anniversaries that's really a monthiversary (Clara's idea, of course) and the original plan was to smoke, screw, sleep, and eat to our heart's content. I was flush, and Clara was keen to spend every dollar I had to my name. I didn't mind. She was one hell of a distraction, as far as distractions go, and I could think of a lot worse things to do than drop all my cash on a weekend of debauchery with the highest earning night time act at the Purple Armadillo.

Anyway, I woke up close to midnight to a call of nature, and noticed this weird light flashing from the edges of the blackout curtains. At first I thought it might be cops or something, but the colors were all wrong. Green, purple, orange; not cop colors at all, so I pulled back the curtains and took a peek.

The colors were everywhere, touched *everything*, like the sky was full of burning candy. I opened the door to get a better look, and the colors flooded the room. And I don't mean that they came in like normal light. No, these colors flowed past and around me like smoke swirling through a projector beam.

Clara grunted and opened her eyes, told me to shut the door before seeing the smoke light and bolting upright in the bed. She sat there waving her arms in front of her dreamily, running her fingers through the cloud, splitting it into soft tendrils over and over. I watched her, transfixed, her nude form bathed in kaleidoscope.

Hard as it was, I turned away, wandered outside in my boxers. There was a small group gathered in the center of the parking lot, their faces turned upward, mouths gaping. I joined them, lifting my own head to see what they were gawking at. I nearly fell over from shock.

There was a rip in the sky. The starfield had been torn open, revealing a churning, white Void from which the colors were bleeding.

Being birthed from this Void was a giant puppet's head; wriggling, thrashing, working its jaws silently up and down, like a great, yarny worm burrowing its way free from some extra-dimensional prison.

At some point Clara, wrapped in the comforter, touched my elbow, breaking me out of a minutes-long reverie. Without hesitation I grabbed her wrist and led her back into the hotel, locking the door behind us.

I stood with my head against the door, my back to the room. Clara's breaths behind me were ragged and heavy to match my own. Turning, the first thing I saw was that she had gotten dressed, but then noticed her arm outstretched, finger pointing at the wall in front of the bed. I looked to see that instead of a television resting precariously upon a dilapidated old dresser, there was instead a set of chrome elevator doors.

I barely managed a clumsy "What the hell?" before Clara started toward the door hypnotically, lining her pointing finger up with the call button resting beside those impossible doors.

"No!" I cried, reaching for her, but my feet sank into the floor as if it were made of sponge. I fell headfirst into the carpet, sinking several inches down. She pressed the button. A loud whirring sounded. The doors opened with a warbled ping. Multicolored light tumbled out.

She turned and looked down at me. "What are you doing?" she asked, her voice trancelike. "We have to go." She stepped into the elevator, pressing her hand against the side to prevent the doors from closing.

My mind wouldn't focus. I couldn't form words. There was nothing but to follow, so I did.

The inside of the elevator was glass, and beyond the panes was our city, irrevocably changed. Skyscrapers pulsed like parasitic worms escaping from the eyes of a dead snail. The streets flowed like liquid, lapping up and over their curbs. People were gathered, standing ankle-deep in those streets, every one of them gazing skyward. I looked up with them, just as I had done in the parking lot, to once again see the puppet dominating the sky, its sock-like body undulating as well, its mouth constantly working.

A calm came over me, like one feels when dreaming, confronted by things that can not be real, yet are accepted as such. "This must be a dream," I said to Clara, who laughed.

"Can't be a dream. I'm here too," she said, through her mirth.

"That doesn't prove anything."

She just kept giggling.

"Why are you laughing?" I asked her, but she kept going.

The elevator doors closed, and we began to descend. Clara pressed her whole body against the glass, looking up and down and side to side manically. I had a vivid notion of her falling through—cut to ribbons, tumbling to her death—and tried to pull her away, but she wouldn't budge.

She jerked her elbow from my grip and continued to work her head spasmodically.

"The puppet, it's Zilch!" she said.

"Who?"

"Zilch the Strange, from the Dr. Buttons Show."

"I don't know what that is," I replied.

"He was Dr. Buttons' sidekick. I watched that show every afternoon after school when I was a kid. I used to love the silly way Zilch laughed. *Hyuck, hyuck, hyuck, Dr. B.* You never watched Dr. Buttons?"

"No," I said, trying to pull her away again.

"You really missed out, then."

She pulled herself out of my hand once more.

The elevator stopped, the doors opened. We both turned and looked through the portal to see the bullpen of a large office, akin to the inside of a call center. Hundreds of unmanned telephones rested on desks that seemed to go on forever. Chairs were scattered, computer monitors upturned, some hanging off their desks, CRT heads cleaved from digital bodies. Paper littered every surface. Shreds of it danced in the air. It was as though a bomb had gone off.

Clara finally peeled herself off the elevator window. We stepped into the office together. The doors closed behind us, and when I looked back, they were gone, nothing but a blank wall where they had been.

"I used to work here," said Clara.

"You what? When?"

"Right after I dropped out of college. My uncle got me the job." She ran away from me, across the room and down one of the exploded isles. "This was my station. We cold-called people, tried to sell them security systems." She reached down, picked up the receiver of the work station's phone, put it to her ear. "Good evening, Mr. Whats-i-doo. Sorry to interrupt your dinner, but would you be interested in scheduling an appointment with one of our top-notch, home security experts today?" Clara dropped the handset, started giggling like an idiot again.

Every phone in the office went off at once. Over and over they rang, until Clara retrieved the receiver and placed it back to the side of her head.

"Hello," she said quietly.

The phone speakers buzzed to life. A high, thin, staticky voice blasted out of them. "Dr. Buttons is retiring today. There's cake in the break room. Come and get it. I repeat, there's break in the cake room, a break in the cake room. Come get your fill before it's too late. Hyuck, hyuck, hyuck."

"Zilch . . ." said Clara, then dashed away toward the back of the office.

"Wait!" I cried, and chased after.

She ran down several interconnected hallways—left, then right, then left again, over and over—filled with doors and frosted windows. Shadowy, wavy forms inside the offices pressed smudgy faces and hands against the cloudy glass. Indistinct chatter poured out from behind the doors; one long, muddied conversation that oozed into my ears and left my head addled.

Finally, we reached the end of our mad dash. Clara stood before a door at the dead end of the last hallway. A banner hung across the door with the words *"Retyremint Partee!!!"* smeared across it in red paint. Four-fingered handprints surrounded the misspelled scrawl.

"This is it," she said. "The cake room." She opened the door.

That description proved to be more than apt. Inside, the room was top to bottom covered in icing. The smell was sickening,cloying. I retched. I could see several dozen fully clothed mannequins gathered in a semi-circle, their blank faces posed to look down on something obscured by Clara's body.

Clara stepped in without hesitation, her feet instantly sinking into the confection, all the way up to her ankles. She raised her knees, pulling her feet out one at a time with a quiet sucking sound, and made her way over to a table resting in the center of the room. I followed, stepping carefully. The spaces between my toes filled with cold icing and warm cake.

I joined Clara beside the table. On top of it lay the body of a balding, middle-aged man dressed in a brown suit. His arms were crossed over his chest, and his eyes were closed behind round, wire-rimmed glasses.

"My Uncle Bernard," she half-whispered, touching the lapel tentatively.

"The one that got you the job?"

"Yeah. But he died last year. He looked just like this when they laid him out."

"I'm sorry," I replied stupidly.

"Don't be. He was a piece of shit. Used to babysit me for my mother after school. Take me down into his basement to "play" after my cartoons. Sick fuck." She snorted, and then spit a green glob onto the face of the body. Its skin distorted as the phlegmy discharge ran down. Without thinking, I reached out to touch the distortion, but she grabbed my hand.

"Don't. It's just icing; more cake."

The mannequin closest to us, one dressed in a black tuxedo, raised its hand, which had a silver cake server taped to it.

"I guess you get to cut the cake," I said.

Clara smacked the hand of the mannequin, dislodging its arm, which slid out of the sleeve and splattered onto the cake floor. She screamed, bringing both her fists up above her head. She pushed them together at the wrists, and then smashed them down into the head of the cake corpse, exploding it into pieces of red and pink. She scooped handfuls of the body out, threw them at the mannequins over and over, until every one was askew and the Uncle Bernard cake was nothing more than a mass of baked gore.

A speaker in the upper left corner of the room exploded with the sound of the voice from the telephone, the one Clara identified as "Zilch."

"Now, now, you cow. Gifts are supposed to be enjoyed, not destroyed. But it's okay if you don't want to play. Someone else can take a turn. Hyuck, hyuck, hyuck."

The floor gave way beneath us, and we were sucked into a cakehole to tumble through a howling, black abyss.

Eventually, I landed hard on my back, elbow deep in grass. Above me, the puppet was there, still working its sock mouth.

"Must be one big foot," I said deliriously and laughed.

"What do you mean," asked Clara from my right.

I sat up, seeing that we were lying in a large open field dotted with marigolds.

"The puppet, it kind of looks like a big sock. I was just thinking about how big a foot must have gone in it once."

"It's not a sock. It's Zilch. He's a ventriloquist's dummy."

I looked up again, and back to Clara. "Looks like a sock to me."

"You're wrong."

"Whatever. It's different for me, I guess." I stood up, stretched, then ran my feet back and forth in the grass, attempting to get as much icing and cake off as I could.

Clara stood up as well. "Where are we now?"

I gave it another survey. It took me no time to realize.

"Rabbit Run."

"Rabbit Run?"

"Yeah. I used to spend summers here with my Grandpa Willy. After my grandma died, he moved out to the country. Called his place Rabbit Run, because of all the wild rabbits on the land. He used to take me out to hunt them. 'To keep 'em off the flowers,' he said. Don't really have a stomach for killing, though. Could never pull the trigger. He called me Little Pussy my whole life because of it."

"So he was an asshole?"

"Yeah. Used to stand behind me while I aimed, then crack me on the head with his knuckles when I wouldn't shoot."

I turned in a circle, looking for Grandpa Willy's house, but it wasn't there. Instead, on the horizon, was a concrete structure far in the distance, stretching tall and ominous.

"I guess we go there."

"Sure. What else?" she said, shrugging.

We'd barely taken a step before the ground churned around us; exploded. Grass and dirt flew into the air and rained down on our heads. The air fluttered with yellow petals. Thousands of decaying rabbit bodies pulled themselves up and out of the ground, began scrabbling around the field. A crack resounded through the air, unmistakable. A gunshot.

"Run, rabbits. RUN!" Grandpa Willy. Behind us.

We both turned to look, and there he was, looming at the edge of the distant treeline. He stood half as tall as the tallest of those trees, twelve feet if he was an inch, dressed just like I remember: overalls without a shirt, an overlarge hat covering his head, and of course, no shoes or socks to be found. "Just as the good Lord intended," he used to say.

Delirium overtook me at the sight of my giant grandfather. "Big foot," I said again, and laughed, though I still don't know why.

He aimed his enormous rifle in our direction.

"I said run, Little Pussy! Take your bitch and get to gettin.'"

"I think we should do what he says," said Clara, over the squeals of the dead rabbits. She grabbed at my arm, pulled it hard.

"Nah, he's a shit shot," I said, still drunk on whatever spell the place had put me under. "We got time."

Another crack, and a giant bullet wooshed past us, exploding the bodies of about ten undead bunnies as it hit the ground with a loud "WUMPH."

This broke me out of my stupor.

"Okay, let's go," I said.

And we were running.

The ground boiled around our ankles. Rabbit bones melted together into a tar-like consistency, slurping as we sank into it. I could feel wet teeth scratching against my shins, gooey eyeballs popping under my heels. We had to pull one another out of the muck several times. Giant bullets shattered the air and field in front of us. At one point, I dared to look over my shoulder. Grandpa Willy strode not far behind, his legs lengthening impossibly with each

erik mchatton

153

extension. Those great, bare feet of his slapped the ground. I could see bits and pieces of liquified rabbit carcasses and marigolds stuck between his toes, dripping onto the ground in black, red, and yellow blobs.

"Gonna getcha,'" he cried, raising his gun once more and letting another blast fly, which I could feel against my ear as it passed and landed just inches in front of us. "Gonna get me a Little Pussy. Two for the price of one! Hyuck, hyuck, hyuck."

I picked Clara up, threw her over my shoulder, then pumped my way through the rabbity quagmire as hard as I could, desperately trying to reach the concrete behemoth looming larger and larger at the end of the field. Somehow I knew if I managed that, ole Willy couldn't follow.

Clara, bouncing on my shoulder, eyes no doubt increasingly full of my grandfather, kept yelling "Hurry," as if I didn't already know, and just when I thought I could feel Willy's hot breath and tobacco spit on my neck, my feet came down on solid asphalt.

I sat Clara down, turned in a circle, only to find no Willy, no dead rabbit field; nothing but dreadful silence, and an expanse of parking spaces that went on into forever—a solid gray horizon; the concrete building its only feature, rupturing out of the ground like a tumor. The building was cube shaped, and windowless, except for a set of double red doors in its center. There were no markings to indicate what type of building it was. Its true nature scratched at my brain, needled me with ghostly memory.

Without thinking, I looked to the sky. The puppet was there, socky jaws working, the only constant in the now inconstant world.

I plucked an eyeball from Clara's shoulder, and flicked it onto the ground. She laughed, quietly, and put a hand on my cheek. Rubbing her thumb and forefinger across, she brought them away: there were two tiny buck teeth, pinched between her nails. I laughed along with her. Staring at one another we let our laughter overtake us for a bit—what else could we do?—before finally turning our attention to the structure.

We approached the doors cautiously. Clara grabbed one handle, I the other. We pulled them open at the same time.

The air that rushed out to meet us was stagnant, with a fake floral finish. The kind of air you might find inside an old woman's apartment, or the vestibule of a dying hotel. I couldn't make out what waited beyond; the inside was too dim. Clara stepped in first, disappeared into the darkness. I briefly entertained the insane idea of closing the doors behind her, consigning her to whatever fate awaited within that dully familiar place; but of course, I followed, if only because I seemed to have no other choice.

It took my eyes a moment to adjust. I blinked over and over until the room polaroided itself into sense. I found myself in a waiting room full of hard plastic orange chairs welded together at their bases. Sitting in these chairs were dolls, ragamuffins, the kind you sometimes see kids playing with in old movies. Some were slumped, heads forward, between their legs; others to the side, arms over their chests, legs splayed out in front. Each doll was the size you'd expect from something designed for a child, except one. In the far right corner was one of full human size. It sat rigid, stumpy hands holding a clipboard, half the wooly brown hair intermittently missing from its head. The doll in the seat next was reaching across, clutching onto its leg. Its head rested on the lap of the bigger doll.

A cold chill ran down my spine. I knew them. I remembered them. I was there so many times. The big doll was my grandmother. The little one, me: my shiny Buster Browns dangling over the seat, my red wagon overalls buttoned on only one side, just like I liked it. This was the waiting room of the place my granny used to go for chemotherapy. She would bring me along since my mother worked during the day. Tears welled in my eyes. I had an overwhelming urge to go and throw the little doll out of its chair and take its place, to clutch on to my granny again after all these years. Instead, I turned to Clara.

She was on the ground, on her knees. Her face was ashen. Her mouth moved up and down without sound, reminding me of the puppet. I squatted, grabbed her shoulders.

"What's wrong?"

"Do you know where this is?" she asked me, looking into my eyes with an emotion somewhere between anger and shame.

"I do. This is where my grandmother came for chemo, for all the good it did her."

"No, that's not right. This is the waiting room of Patterson Women's Health Clinic, Dunnstown North."

"The...wait, what? No, this is St. Bartholomew's Cancer Center in Kingsport."

She grabbed my arms and stood up.

"What color is the wallpaper?" she asked.

"No wallpaper. The walls are painted beige."

"There is wallpaper. Baby blue with yellow flowers. I'll never forget it."

"So we're seeing it differently, like the puppet."

"I guess so."

She walked around the room slowly, touching the backs of every chair. She sat down in one, right on top of a doll, like it wasn't there. The doll squished and then popped with a puff of air, disappearing beneath her.

I joined her, picking up the blond haired doll in the chair beside her. I set it gently on the floor.

"So, a cancer hospital for me, and an abortion clinic for you. That's just . . . that's . . ."

"Fucking sick, is what it is. This is all one big, sick joke. First that job with my uncle, and now this."

"You don't see the dolls, do you?"

"Dolls?"

"There's dolls in all the chairs. There's even one over in the corner that looks like my granny, and one beside her that looks like me."

She glanced over at where I pointed.

"No, the chairs are empty."

"Ahhh. See, they were always full when I was here. I used to sit and think about all those people being sick, like my grandmother. I wondered if they had kids that would miss them too."

"I was never lonelier than I was in this room, sitting by myself," said Clara, wiping her eyes and nose with the back of her sleeve.

Clara grabbed my hand, held it against her face. I put my head against hers, kissed her cheek. We sat there like that, comforting each other in pain long passed and found again—until a loud voice blared out over the intercom.

"*Calling Doctor Howard, Doctor Fine, Doctor Howard. I repeat: calling Doctor Howard, Doctor Fine, Doctor Howard. Hyuck, hyuck, hyuck.*"

"It's mocking us," I said.

"FUCK YOU!" Clara screamed at the ceiling.

The door beside the empty reception desk opened, and a figure came through. Its body was human shaped, wearing a crisp, white lab coat over a brown suit, but the head was decidedly not human. It was the head of the puppet, giant sock face sticking out of the collar, googly eyes rolling.

Zilch.

"No, no. Fuck youuuuuuu!" said Zilch, pointing at Clara. Then it laughed, and laughed, and laughed, holding its belly with one arm while keeping its other up and pointing.

Behind it, then, ducking through the doorway, came two hulking nurses. They advanced on us slowly, their round, shiny heads and black, featureless faces like unfinished drawings. Clara stood up and started toward them, an insane fury in her eyes, but I could see crushing death in their fat, four fingered hands, so I shot after her, grabbed her, pulled her around the brutes, who awkwardly lunged to stop us. We bowled through the sock doctor, pushing it into the wall. It was still laughing as I ran through the door, deeper into the offices. Clara, in tow, was still screaming a practically incoherent stream of profanities over her shoulder.

Doors upon doors zoomed by as we ran. There were voices coming from behind them that sounded like someone talking when you're not listening. It was the same murky conversation as before, back in the hallways of Clara's old office. It sounded as if it was getting closer, both in distance and comprehension. I was instantly afraid of what would happen should I ever understand what those voices were saying.

The hallway ended in a stairwell, and Clara pushed past me to go through when I hesitated. She made it halfway down the first flight before turning around.

"What are you doing? We have to go!" she said.

I couldn't move.

"What if it's worse?" I asked.

"What if what's worse?"

"Whatever is down there. Another sock-headed man, a cake room, melting rabbits, giant grandpas, rooms with wallpaper and no wallpaper at the same time. Christ, Clara, I don't think I can bear any more."

She eased back up the stairs and grabbed my hands.

"We're still together. We're still real. That's something, right?"

I nodded, slowly.

"Then let's go. Whatever it is, we'll face it together, okay?"

I took a deep breath. "Okay."

We started down the stairs.

The stairwell was fairly normal, thankfully. The only thing was that it became narrower, the deeper we went. At first, I tried to convince myself that I was imagining it, but we kept descending, flight after flight, until I began to feel that when we reached the bottom, we might be greeted by hell itself. Eventually, though, we did reach the end, and huddled together in front of a tall door marked "Exit," on a step that was no more than a foot and a half wide. Just like before, we looked at one another, and then, as one, opened the door.

On the other side was a vast, empty place, walls and floors made of pulsating pink flesh, containing car-like things made of the same.

This is when I first felt you.

Clara let go of my hand, wandered away from me. That is when we disconnected completely.

I could feel myself being watched; prickles on the back of the neck, scalp tingling, filled with an overwhelming urge to find the eyes I felt upon me. There was nothing and no one, just Clara and I in that strange, empty place that reminded me of a parking garage.

Clara moved to the nearest car, then opened its door.

"C'mon," she said, her voice faraway.

My feet moved, and an awful sensation of not being in control came over me, as if my legs were being worked by invisible strings. I got in the car, felt the cold, meaty seat against my bare skin. The door closed of its own accord. The car started, rolled backward out of the parking space.

We were off.

Round and round we went, passing countless other meat cars, all of which contained one or more passengers, all blurry and indistinct. Upon reaching the end, we stopped at a structure that resembled a ticket booth. Hanging out of the booth was a hamburger faced construction crammed into a jumpsuit, two giant plastic googly eyes without pupils pressed into its soft head. It had a paper sign around its neck, soaked in red, and the name "Stevie" scrawled across it in uneven black letters. Its hand was out, four-fingered and plump. A speaker by the thing's head buzzed and Zilch's voice came through.

"Tickets puh-leeze, hyuck, hyuck, hyuck."

The glove box fell open. Two slices of an unrecognizable meat with black squiggles all over fell out and onto Clara's lap. She handed them to me, a strange glazed look in her eye, and I placed them, autonomically, into "Stevie's" meaty paw.

"Thanks a big ole bunch. Now, buckle up, buckaroos!"

The car sped away, tires spinning, squelching, filling the cab with the smell of cooked pork.

We pulled from the parking lot and into a great dark, fleshy tunnel, just large enough for our car to pass through. Everything went black. I lost sensation, could no longer feel the seat against my body. A sense of non-being enveloped me. I tried to scream, to prove I still existed. I couldn't.

My arms reached up and grabbed the steering wheel without me asking them to. The sensation of its slimy solidity brought relief. That I could feel something again emboldened me, and with great effort I managed to wrest some control away from whatever force now dominated me.

I whispered Clara's name, but she did not respond. I thought for sure she was no longer there.

The car began to slow, and I heard the sides squishing against the walls. The antiseptic reek of ozone began to mix with the coppery scent that permeated the interior of the strange vehicle. Then, there was a light; dull and yellow at first, then abruptly bright, blinding white.

We exited the tunnel—squeezed out with a *splorch*—and bounced onto the rabbit eye, marigold road, back at the beginning and the end, right where we started, you and I.

We're nearly there now. The closer we get, the sense that we've done this before becomes stronger. My story repeated, again. I can feel you more with each passing minute, out there, listening to my words—which sound like your voice—inside that great dark abyss between your ears. Though your face may change, though you may not be the you you were when last we met, you're still the same as ever: A consumer, consuming me; creating me; torturing me.

Puppet and puppet master, keeping on and on.

The car detaches from the ground, rises into the sky, as it always does. The puppet is growing larger and larger in the windshield. A voice comes over the radio. It's good old Zilch, singing that same old song, a chestnut my father used to play for me during car rides on rare visits.

Welcome back, my friends, to the show that never ends. We're so glad you could attend. Come inside! Come inside.

How many times now?

How many more to go?

I look over to Clara and she's shimmering, off in her own strange story, no doubt. She's lost to me, of course. I wonder if I ever had her to begin with.

At least it isn't you. Like I said before, as long as it isn't, then I believe we both have a chance. As long as I'm in here, and you're out there, and the puppet isn't in your sky, I think we'll be okay.

But eventually it will come for you, like it came for us. It'll come and torture you with all the things you wish never were, force you to tell tumbled together tragedies forever.

I know this because it's telling me to tell you. It thinks it's funny for you to know. Hyuck, hyuck, hyuck.

What will your puppet look like, I wonder?

I'm going in now. The sock mouth is open. The yarny darkness beckons.

Until next time, whoever you are.

the halls

CHRISTI NOGLE

Fiona's hotel room was not ready yet, so she checked her bags at the front desk and gave Brady a call. He was kind enough to come meet her in the lobby. His swagger was new to her, but it made sense based on his online persona. She recognized his signature hairstyle—somewhere between a shag and a mullet—only she hadn't imagined it being red, not at all. He'd only ever posted black-and white-shots, so she had visualized his hair being brown like her own.

The red made her pause, made her feel faint for a second. She could not work out why.

They'd been interacting on social media for some time. Brady had mentioned the outdoor arts-and-crafts fair in his city many times, and this year Fiona had somehow managed both to afford the trip and to subdue her anxiety enough for travel. She was here! He hugged her gently in celebration.

All but spoken during their online conversations was the idea that he might like to feature some of her work in the gallery. She'd been trying not to get her hopes too high, but oh, she fondly wished for it. She wished for more—to move here, to find her real life and her people here.

Now he said, "Let's get some lunch," and on the way he began speaking his plans more clearly. Yes, he wanted to make space for her paintings. Yes, a group show soon, and more to come from that if things went well. She thought she would weep.

They walked to a plain and uninspiring Italian restaurant, then walked a larger loop back to the hotel through a bit of downtown and the park where the festival would be held—just sixteen hours from now.

Fiona mused on how generic spaces had become these days, the smaller cities indistinguishable from one another, all with the same stores and the same clunky architecture. Those aged brick building-fronts could be stamped anywhere. This damp and overheated park seemed like any other. Brady pointed out a piece of public art that looked like a quilt made of tile. He pointed out a fenced-in area for dogs, and further, in the shade, the space where the tents would go up. It all might have been in her own city. Humidity provided the only signal that here was any different from there.

He'd arranged everything for her. The tent and tables he had rented or borrowed. Her boxes of giclée prints and carefully wrapped originals had been delivered to his home. He would bring them in the early morning, and doubtless would stay to help set up. It was all so convenient.

They parted with a second, warmer embrace after they'd established that her hotel room was ready.

Nothing of notice in her room. White, greige, a splash of orange. The bathroom offered blinding light and a wall of mirror. She averted her eyes, wishing she'd trusted Brady enough to stay in the guest room he'd offered. She could not imagine his home but guessed it would be cozy, or stylish, or *something*.

The television would not turn on. She got out of bed to check it was plugged in, considered calling the front desk, but instead lay back again staring at the blank black rectangle.

In the park the next day, people flowed past her tent and into it. Her work hung inside and outside the canvas walls, tiny dark still life paintings in gilt frames, plastic-wrapped prints stacked in a wicker basket. Some of the visitors bought; many more asked stupid questions: Where did she get her inspiration? How long had she been at this?

Brady was part of the arts commission or some such and had duties at their booth, but he sent underlings to give her a break from time to time, to watch her wares. Then she wandered. There was nothing surprising. A lot of rustic-looking pottery, metal lawn sculptures, other painters' work that reminded her of the painting above the hotel bed. A strong waft of butter and cinnamon enticed her to buy a paper cone of roasted pecans, but they had no flavor, and when she'd wandered away from the stand far enough to lose the scent as well, she pitched them into the trash.

Brady and the people he'd brought by had kept saying they'd meet up for drinks, after the booths had been disassembled on the last night. She'd imagined going to his gallery, or someplace a little seedy, or someplace a little swanky, or *something*, but they only met up at the hotel bar. It was vast and greige with a single line of orange neon. The bar and tables were black, covered with fingerprints, sweaty handprints, oily-looking rings where drinks had stood. Brady was busy meeting and greeting. She found herself the focus of a half-circle of arty-looking strangers who kept asking her name, asking what she painted, how long she'd been at it, where she got her ideas.

"From my dreams," she said, and escaped to search for the bathroom.

She found herself in a long hallway. The floor had been something else in the bar, in the room. Some fake gray wood most likely—she could not remember—but here in the hall it was a pinkish marble tile, and that made her feel faint, like Brady's hair had made her feel. A recognition of something she could not quite articulate.

The hall went on and forked, then forked again. She began to clip along more quickly, began to sweat, and then suddenly, there were the bathrooms. A long line at the ladies' and a single person waiting outside the men's, and it was Brady. She approached as quietly as she could so he wouldn't turn. How awkward it would be to meet and talk, and possibly hug, at the bathrooms. She moved slowly behind him toward the line of ladies and noticed his hair was not simply red, as she had thought. It was sable, pale at the roots, going red quickly and then going dark—almost black—at the tips, like the fur of a husky or a fox.

They were saying long goodbyes in the lobby. They'd stayed up too late, all agreed, and it was time to sleep, but no one could quite pull away. *So much fun! So great to see you again; so good to meet you.* Only Fiona was tense, even a little teary.

Here Brady came, setting his eyes on her for the first time all weekend, asking what could be wrong. She would not say, but he knew. She'd wanted to see the gallery, hadn't she?

"How could I have been so—" he groaned and turned. "Everyone, your attention: the night's not over."

They cheered.

The limos came around and they left all together, single-file. They glided through downtown streets and brightly-lit tunnels, all strangely empty.

"How late can it be?" Fiona yelled, but no one could tell her. They were passing around an oversized bottle of champagne.

"Fiona's opening is tonight," Brady said, they cheered, and someone popped another, larger bottle.

The tunnels were made of pinkish marble tile, as were the streets, as were the floors of the gallery. Inside, her paintings had already been hung. It seemed the walls had been painted to suit them—or no, *papered,* in heavy dark cut-velvet. Someone brought out glasses so they could wander more dignified among the paintings rather than passing the bottles.

Every image showed a different cluttered tabletop. The richness of another century. Jewel tones and all the qualities of jewels, dimly lit but entirely overwhelming. The deepest, clearest reds and magentas, deep cobalt blue and peacock blue, and peacock feathers, luster glass, cloisonné trinkets, tables strewn with half-peeled citrus fruits and gutted pomegranates, snarls of necklaces and rings. In the last one, her favorite, light glinted off a silver tray atop a stack of brocades, and on the tray sat a fan made of feathers, an antique glass perfume diffuser, and a boar hairbrush with inlaid abalone handle. The brush was well used and ready for cleaning.

Fiona wandered with the rest, feeling such gratitude, accepting many compliments and overhearing others. She was overwhelmed with the warmth of it all, though when she turned away from the final painting, she was not surprised to see a spotlight turned on her. She was up on a raised platform, which had become like a stage, and her audience stood in the sunken part of the gallery. All of them were grouped before her again in a half-circle, shadowy now and not such strangers anymore, though they were wanting the same thing as before. "Really, Fiona," they said, "where do you get your ideas? Where does all of this splendor come from?"

"And how long have you been at this?"

At first she thought Brady was gone. The gallery had grown so dark, and the spotlight made it feel darker. She caught him back a few paces behind the others, deep in shadow. She watched him remove his suit jacket with a flourish and toss it away.

"You're not going to let me off the hook? It's so late," she said to the crowd.

They only briefly tittered and continued to gaze.

"If you must know, when I was a child I had a fantasy. It was a daydream that leaked into my nightdreams sometimes. I lived in a . . . castle." That wasn't the right word, the right word was maze, but what did she owe these people, really? "There were endless halls made of pink marble tile, and I would walk these halls day and night. At first I was panicked, running, screaming, you know. But as I spent more time there—"

"How much time?" someone said, and another, "How long have you been at this?"

She began to feel that this might take a while to tell. She leaned to set down her champagne glass, and in the same elegant motion, tucked her velvet dress close to her knees to sit on the edge of the platform.

"And what do you mean, a fantasy?" someone said, and another, "And were you alone?"

"Please," she said. "I'll tell you all you want, just let me find my own way in."

It was hard to know where to start. With the crying baby in the room she had tried to represent in these paintings? With the long walks in her neighborhood? Earlier?

She took a sip of champagne. It had no taste, no sting. She chuckled and sniffed. No odor. She breathed deeply, scanned the crowd. Their faces obscured, only their forward-leaning stances belied their eagerness.

She breathed once more and began.

] [

To tell you of The Halls, I have to start a little earlier. The tail end of sixth grade.

I'd taken to walking after dinner every day. I'd gone to Mom and said I was worried about my weight a little and wanted to get stronger. I knew it wasn't healthy to diet, so I thought a little extra walking would be the way to go. I felt her eyes roving over me. *Not an ounce overweight,* she was thinking, *not yet.* She was proud of me for being so on top of things in such a healthy way, but disappointed because that would mean one less hour of assistance with the little ones. After dinner was homework time, after all, and sometimes we started the baths near that time too. The oldest was in second grade, so there wasn't too much homework, but there were so many babies, and I really was a help.

She was always measuring herself—and all of us—against an ideal version. Would the ideal Fiona do this, would her ideal mommy do that?

I'm saying it wrong. I'm making her a cartoon. She was lovely, really, but I had gotten into a bind with her. I had loved it too much. The work, the compliments on the work. *Fiona's so good at this. Look at her; she's made for it.*

I had become as invested in the babies as she was, as Dad was. But they weren't *mine*, and I had begun to think I ought to have something that was.

It hadn't been easy for me. I was bone-tired all the time, without a moment to think, without a social life, just the appearance of one. I wanted time to think; that's all the walks were at first. A time to think about who I'd like to be in the future, to pick out clues of my possible identity from the day's events, from the previous night's dreams.

Our immediate neighborhood was well-kept and bland, just like our house. Nothing out of place but nothing, really, to see, and so I'd rush away as far as I could, even though Mom had warned me to stay within certain confines. I'd see messy yards and strange, aggressive bumper stickers, houses in colors my parents would have found garish, but eventually those things became so familiar they stopped making an impression too, so that I was only walking and thinking. The thinking was supposed to be about what I wanted, but it was always only about escape. The space around me would recede from notice, and at some point it would come back into my consciousness, changed.

I would be in The Halls for a moment, only The Halls were pretending to be something else. *Oh, I wasn't paying attention and I wandered into a tunnel,* I'd think, and it would be so. I walked that first hall a long time to come out the other end realizing it was a pedestrian underpass of some sort, just as I'd rationalized it to be. The traffic roared above as I approached the exit. I walked out into a park much like the one where we spent this past weekend, a park in my city, miles from where I was allowed to be.

Another time, I lost track of where I was and saw the very same thing. Tall plaster walls in a color between gray and beige, a pinkish marble tile floor. A doorless hall eight or ten feet wide, identical to the one before, though I knew I'd gone east from home this time, not west, and had not at any point circled back. *Well, this is odd,* I thought. The hall forked and then forked again. I remembered reading something about mazes but could not remember what it was, and so I chose each turn at random. I was rushing now. Feeling fear—feeling it deeply—and not willing to articulate that, instead I thought, *These must be the back hallways of the shopping mall.* Of course they were! The mall's floor was just like this. Almost as soon as I realized it, I made the final turn toward the exit and heard murmurs of shoppers. I walked out into an ill-used corner of the mall. I noted that the floor was indeed marble tile, but it was grainier and much, much grayer than the tile in The Halls. But then I turned and saw an old woman with a mop enter where I had exited. It wasn't some fantasy place, then; it was only the back hallway, and I had only been panicking.

Though I ran back home—from the park, from the mall, and several other places too—there was no way of denying I had repeatedly stayed out too late. Mom and Dad were saggy-eyed and irritable. The babies fussed and screamed, not getting all they needed with one less parent around.

I had initially hoped to find my people on these walks, though in the two or three years of walking, I never ran into anyone who wasn't boring, vaguely threatening, or more often, both. Still, my parents decided I'd been lying, that I had been getting in with a wrong crowd. They forbade the walks and cheerfully had a Peloton delivered to the primary suite. Now, in the hour after dinner, Dad babysat while I spent one half hour on the bike, one half hour doing Pilates moves on the carpet at the foot of their bed. Mom did the moves first and then the bike, and it was so efficient that way. My parents called it our "girl time" and often remarked on the way it had transformed our shapes.

] [

"How is any of this addressing our questions?" someone said, and another, "Did The Halls have any orange? Any black?"

Fiona had not been aware of the crowd. She had disappeared into her story and they had all receded. Here they were, the people as well as Brady, who had stayed near the back wall but who'd grown much taller. The jacket had gone earlier; the pants had gone too sometime when she'd been lost in her story. Brady was all shadowy soft edges now, all fur.

"Come here," she said, patting her knee.

The being at the back of the room shook his head.

"Please finish," someone said, and another, "It's late. We can't hold on much more."

] [

So, my home felt more and more a prison—my entire life a cell. I worried that I was going to grow up and become Mom, and sometimes I thought I already was her, that 'Fiona' was only a fantasy or hallucination of hers.

Suffice to say there was a lot of repressed strife going on, and a gaping emptiness where my walks had been. That's when Grandmother began to visit. Always from behind me—I never dared to look, but I knew her as the woman I'd seen in the mall, the one with the mop—and she'd suggest things. Beautiful things like you see in my work, all around us here. Colors that had no place in my parents' house, exquisite textures. Iridescence, light through glass. Like that.

She sent me these images in a kind of song, I think. It's so long ago now.

As I gave the sweet babies their baths, she'd stand behind me. As I washed the dishes, folded laundry, made beds. She told me she'd caught a different kind of baby in the woods, a baby monster. A singular, special thing, and I was the one she'd chosen to take care of it because I was so good. I was made for this.

Not just take care of it. I could *have* it. I could live in The Halls forever and have such riches there—for The Halls had doorways after all, few and far between, but doorways opening into dimly lit rooms filled with gorgeous books, filled with fantastical clothes, jewelry, works of art and of nature. Things like I had never seen here, in my little house, in my sad little city. I would have all of that, and I would have the greatest gift of all: my own person.

Fully a person and so much more than a person too, and furry like the pets I'd always longed for, which my parents would never allow in their immaculate home.

It could do so much, my baby. Didn't I want to see how much it could do?

I would see Grandmother outside and look away. On the way to school, she'd open a gate in a wooden fence. I'd rush my siblings past, catching in the corner of my eye the glint of marble tile. When we took the three oldest to the mall for back-to-school, she beckoned from that same opening I had found. She certainly held no mop now. She wore velvet robes and dripped with jewels.

I resisted her temptations until I didn't. A birthday party day, I was set to policing the fun. A truck pulled up, and I thought it was something about the party. A pony, or they were coming too early to take down the bouncy castle. I went to the street to see, and as I approached, the truck's back doors began opening. I caught the old woman's face in the side mirror before I caught the pinkish glow within.

I looked back toward the lawn. Dad and Mom were both there, along with a great many other adults. I was not needed. It was safe to go, and so I took off my party shoes and hoisted myself up into the truck onto the cool tile. I looked back at the placid street and heard the sweet little shrieks of the children until the first fork, and then I didn't hear them any more.

] [

The people murmured amongst themselves.

"Won't you come here," Fiona said, patting her knee again. She laughed and wiped her eyes with the back of her hand.

The being at the back of the room was so large now that he had to stoop to miss the chandelier.

"And turn on the lights, or turn off the spotlight at least," she said. "The show is done."

The chandelier came on just as Brady got down on all fours, something like a Tibetan Mastiff, or Snufalupagus, one of the Wild Things, or one of those long-haired cows, only three times the size of the largest of those. He was still a baby, though—still teething, his horns still blunt.

The crowd saw nothing amiss. "But you haven't answered," someone said, and another, "How long?"

Brady lumbered to the step where Fiona sat. She patted her knee again as though to take all that bulk on her lap, and Brady made a questioning groan.

She'd taught him so much, or tried, but speech was beyond Brady's physiology somehow. Her baby patted his own knee, and Fiona rose to sit there and gaze into his giant human eyes. Once, Brady had been so small that they had held this pose in reverse, and her eyes had been as large to him.

She lost her hands in Brady's soft, deep fur. She had brushed that fur with the boar brush. Turning, she saw it there on the tabletop, not a painting but the thing itself, matted with sable hairs.

She had found him in that first gilded room she came to after the long walk away from the birthday party, but the brush had not appeared until later.

" 'How long have we been at this?,' they wanted to know," she said. "I have no clue, do you?"

Brady shook his head.

It had been a long time. If ever one of these rooms had a mirror, she thought she would recognize the face quite well. No mirror was needed to see the texture of her arms, her hands.

She realized she was dripping with jewels. The bracelets swayed and sparkled. Emerald, ruby, sapphire, and something quite orange. She smiled.

The crowd asked no more questions. They were only a collection of dressmaker dummies in hats and boas, glorious velveteen jackets, and furs, and things like that. The room was littered with empty champagne bottles.

"Will you ever tire of playing pretend?" she said, and the baby shook his head vigorously.

Telepathically, he asked, "Were you playing along this time? I thought maybe. . ."

"Never!" she said, getting up from his knee. "I'm completely convinced, every time. You've gotten so good at it."

Brady settled on all fours again.

"We'll go on, then?"

He nodded. They left the room in ruins, and when they'd gotten through the doorway, she sunk her thin hands into the thick fur of his neck and looped her knee across his arm. He rose slowly so that she could adjust to her customary perch on his shoulders.

Fiona rode through the Halls instead of walking, now. Far above the marble floors, she rode on the massive beast she had raised and nurtured. They searched for the next room, the next playtime, thinking all their conversations rather than saying them. She never was unhappy, never thought of escape, never thought of the other life—or the other lives— she might have lived.

How could she think of such things, when he heard every thought?

the barrow-keeper

NINA SHEPARDSON

With an effort, Edmund pushed himself to his feet. "Damn Richard and his emus."

He lifted the mangled bird feeder off its hook. Most of the seed inside was gone, but a trickle of sunflower and millet spilled out from the plastic tube. After carrying it inside and throwing it in the trash can, Edmund sat down at his computer to compose an email to his neighbor.

Two sentences in, Edmund realized Richard was likely to blow off the email unless he provided evidence that an escaped emu was indeed to blame. He could just imagine Richard leaning against the fence between the cemetery and his emu farm, telling a story about his friend's cousin whose bird feeder had been knocked down by a bear. Edmund levered himself up from his chair and went outside to take some photos of the footprints that surrounded the former site of the feeder. They were unmistakably avian, with three spindly, clawed toe-prints. They were also as large as his own footprints.

Armed with photographic evidence, Edmund returned to his email. "Should such incidents continue," he finished, "I will have no choice but to inform the corporate office." He hovered his mouse over "Send" and stabbed the left button.

Richard's runaway emu, while annoying and destructive, was at least an innocent animal. It had destroyed the bird feeder because its instincts drove it to search for food, not out of malice. The same, however, couldn't be said for the other intruders to the cemetery.

Edmund's shoulders slumped as he remembered the initials he'd found carved into the birch tree growing from Danielle Ortega's grave. The sap dripping from the deep gashes in the white bark looked like blood seeping from a wound. This was no robust old oak; only time would tell if the wound dealt to the young tree would prove as mortal as the illness that had struck Danielle down in her prime.

] [

Ed,

Look, I know you don't like my emus. But come on. They're all where they're supposed to be, and there are no holes in the fence. Whatever wrecked your feeder, it wasn't them, and a bunch of fake prints aren't going to convince anyone.

I don't even understand why you're so upset. You're the caretaker for a green cemetery, for Christ's sake! The whole point is to memorialize the dead without pumping them full of chemicals that'll leach into the groundwater and plant more trees to soak up some extra CO2, right? Can't you see I'm trying to make things better too? Emus don't need nearly as much space as cows, so you don't have to turn a billion acres of prairie into grazing pastures for them.

Please stop harassing me about this. I don't want to cause trouble for you, but if you keep faking evidence to blame me with, I'm not going to have any choice.

—Richard

Edmund ran a hand through his thinning hair. Faking evidence? Apparently, Richard thought Edmund had oodles of free time that he could use to build fake emu feet. Calling him 'Ed,' he could forgive. At least it wasn't 'Eddie.' But this conspiracy theory bullshit? What next, the footprints were really made by emu-shaped aliens?

Edmund left his office and stomped along the paths between the trees. His subordinates had done a good job of mowing the grass. He moved from grave to grave, removing wilted flowers, straightening flags, and inspecting newly-planted saplings. The tension drained out of him as he worked, and even the aches that had more to do with age than frustration eased.

Then he came to Giancarlo Ranucci's grave.

Giancarlo's gravestone was a simple cross, but Edmund thought his tree was one of the most beautiful in the whole cemetery. On his previous rounds, the heady fragrance from the young sapling's single cluster of tiny blossoms had permeated the air. Now, the flowers lay crushed into the grass at the tree's base, along with a scattering of leaves that had been ripped from their branches. It was good luck that the vandals hadn't marked the trunk, but Edmund still wondered if, with so many of its leaves gone, the tree would be able to store up enough energy to survive the next winter.

His hands shook as he ran them over the ash's smooth gray bark. He could only imagine the tirade his grand-mother, God rest her soul, would have launched into if any of the boys in the town he'd grown up in had dared to do such a thing. Her reverence for the dead had extended even to the strangely regular, oblong hills that his parents said were the gravesites of ancient kings and warriors. Barrows, his grandmother had called them, and warned him to stay away. She allowed how what his parents said was true, but she claimed they were also the gathering-places of people who'd lived in Ireland before people came.

"How can there have been people here before people came?"

"They were other people. Not humans. Some folk called them gods. But when our ancestors came here, they drove those old gods underground. They live under the barrows now, with the dead."

It had startled him to hear his grandmother, who was more Catholic than the Pope, speak of 'old gods.' Especially since she seemed to think that they still existed somehow and would punish anyone who trespassed on the barrows. *"They guard those places,"* she'd said.

As he stared at the denuded tree, Edmund wished those grave-guardians were real. *I need you,* he thought, and isn't that pretty much the essence of any prayer?

] [

Edmund watched as Barbara strapped the trail cam to the tree trunk. This wasn't one of the trees that were planted on top of the graves, but a sturdier oak, alongside one of the cemetery's paths.

Barbara stepped back and tucked a strand of her graying hair behind her ear. "That should do it," she said.

The camera faced away from the path, its gaze trained on the section of the cemetery where the incursions had taken place.

"Thanks, Barb," Edmund said. "How much do I owe you for the camera?"

"You don't owe me anything," Barbara said firmly. She put a hand on Edmund's shoulder. "I won't have those hooligans messing with Eric's resting place. Besides, you took care of him when he passed. So now, I'm going to take care of you."

] [

Edmund rubbed his eyes. Five nights of watching and still nothing.

For the first week after Barbara had installed the trail cam, he'd been content to let it record overnight while he slept peacefully at home. All he needed was footage of the vandals he could bring to the police. But no one had snuck into the cemetery at night. (Except maybe Richard's supposedly nonexistent escaped emu, since there were still giant bird footprints around where the bird feeder used to be.)

Edmund had found he couldn't sleep. He laid awake at night, wondering if this was the night the troublemakers would come back. Whose tree would they carve up this time? Clarinda Claremont, the twelve-year-old girl who'd died of leukemia? Adrian Eagleton, a Korean War veteran? Barbara's husband Eric?

Five nights ago, he had come back to the cemetery after dinner. He brought a book with him and stayed up reading while he watched the camera feed from the corner of his eye.

On the second night, he'd put the book down around one in the morning and watched until dawn.

On the third night, he gave up the pretense of reading altogether.

Still, the miscreants hadn't come.

Edmund closed his eyes while he gave voice to a huge yawn, and when he opened them, there was movement on the feed. Three people—young men, it looked like—were climbing over the fence that separated the cemetery from a suburban street.

Edmund knew he should just let the trail cam capture footage and then give it to the police in the morning, but he kept remembering what his grandmother had said about the old gods of Ireland living underground with the dead. The leaves of the trees outside rustled, and he imagined Clarinda and Adrian and Eric shaking the roots wrapped around their bodies, vibrations traveling up through the trunks and making the branches tremble. He heard words in the crackling. *Save us, save us, save us.*

Edmund scooped up a flashlight and left his office. His feet crunched on the gravel paths as he made his way through the cemetery. Outside the illumination of the flashlight's beam, wavering shadows gave the illusion of figures running through the trees.

The patter of the tree branches surrounded him, now punctuated by chirps, twitters, and whistles. Probably the light had disturbed some roosting birds.

It occurred to Edmund that the intruders might be belligerent, especially if they were drunk, but his righteous indignation wouldn't let him return to the office. He gripped the handle of the flashlight, solid and cold and heavy in his hand.

Edmund frowned. He should have reached the area where he'd seen the boys by now. He swept the flashlight beam across the graves, using them to orient himself. He recognized that birch, that maple, the larger spruce between them . . . but where had that willow come from? Willows needed to be near water; he was sure there wasn't any in the cemetery.

The awakened birds grew louder and more numerous. Edmund heard a crow's harsh caw and the wild screech of a hawk. At the same time, the scents of heather and peat wafted on a cool breeze. A wave of nostalgia swept over Edmund, followed by a wave of unease. Those were the smells of his grandmother's home in rural Ireland. What were they doing here, in the American suburbs?

Another sound cut through the birdsong: two men laughing. Edmund's steps faltered. He should be almost on top of them, but they sounded far away. He shook his head. He couldn't let himself get distracted. He was tired, angry, and worried. That was surely a sufficient explanation for anything strange. He oriented himself by the landmarks he recognized and strode on in pursuit of the vandals.

The cries of the birds continued to accompany Edmund on his quest, but the tenor of the human noises in the graveyard changed. The laughter broke off. "What the—" The exclamation was followed by a wordless shout.

"Where are all these fucking birds coming from?" someone demanded.

Now, Edmund could see shifting light through the trees. The vandals had brought flashlights of their own, but the beams bobbed wildly, as if the people holding them were waving their arms around. A yell of pain cut through the general confusion. The erratic light caught something flapping into the trees, and one of the men called, "Shit! My eye!"

Edmund sped up, his own light bouncing over the ground. He came out onto open ground, neat rows of gravestones marked by saplings.

The three men he'd seen on camera staggered around a grave from which a young hawthorn sprung. A swirling mass surrounded them, dipping and wheeling. At first, Edmund thought it was a cloud of bats, but the scene resolved when he remembered what one of the interlopers had said about birds.

Most of them were the kinds of birds American popular culture would condition you to expect in a graveyard. Psychopomps and witches' familiars, Poe's tormentor and Odin's companions. The crows and their larger cousins were shadows, only visible when they crossed the beams of the flashlights. The owls were paler but the absolute silence of their flight made them just as eerie.

As Edmund watched, dumbfounded, others joined them. He saw flashes of fire-engine red and brilliant blue: cardinals and jays. Tiny, drab brown shapes: sparrows and finches. The hawk he'd heard before, white-bellied and red-tailed. The birds dove at the living men who'd trespassed in this place of the dead, stabbing with their beaks and raking with their claws. They seemed to have put aside the distinctions between nocturnal and diurnal, not to mention predator and prey.

One by one, the interlopers dropped their flashlights in favor of covering their heads with their arms. This left only Edmund's steadier light to illuminate the scene, and he realized there were four figures, not three, present. He had originally mistaken it as part of the grave marker it stood beside, a large and ornate one featuring nearly life-sized statues of the Blessed Virgin and the Apostle John flanking the Cross. This fourth figure had no wings, but the soft, russet substance covering most of its body was feathers, not hair or fur. Its legs ended in three-toed bird feet, and its eyes were golden and perfectly round. A circle of wrens hopped and twittered around it.

Edmund remembered his grandmother's talk of the old gods who still guarded the barrows. They were glamorous and enchanting—metaphorically as well as literally—but they were dangerous, too. People might run afoul of them without understanding the significance of what they were doing. He dropped his gaze from the barrow-keeper's yellow eyes. Should he thank it for its aid? Remain silent, to emulate the speechlessness of the dead it must be used to?

A new sound rose over the vocalizations of the birds and the cries of the men. Thumping and rumbling, approaching from the direction of Richard's ranch.

A jolt of horror ran through Edmund. Anyone who'd defile a grave deserved to be frightened, even hurt. But emus stood six feet tall and sported wicked claws on their feet. They were basically velociraptors with feathers.

This was part of the stories, too. The old gods might give someone a gift, only for the recipient to discover it had some unexpected downside.

"Stop!" he called out, and then, remembering how unwise it was to be impolite to such beings, he added, "Please!"

The grave-guardian tilted its head to the side and blinked.

The intruders were trying to flee back in the direction they'd come from, but they stumbled under the onslaught of the birds. A large, brown shape wove through the graveyard, slaloming around granite crosses and angels.

"Watch out!" Edmund called, and the old god tilted its head the other way. Did it not understand him, or was it just confused about why he was helping the people he'd begged it to smite?

All three men turned to see the emu barreling toward them. One man, whose hair was longer than the other two, pulled another—wearing a leather jacket—out of the way. At the same moment, the third man, who stood head and shoulders above the other two, tried to push Leather Jacket back between the emu and himself. Thanks to Long Hair, Leather Jacket wasn't where he expected him to be, and the tall man overbalanced as his hands passed through empty air. He fell into the path of the rampaging emu as his two companions disappeared into the night.

Edmund saw other emus coming in behind the first one. *Dammit, Richard,* he thought reflexively, though he knew his neighbor couldn't have anticipated this. His legs trembled, caught between the competing instincts of freezing and running.

One of the emus emitted a thrumming sound, somewhere between a drumroll and a rumble of thunder. That noise, rolling through his bones, broke Edmund's paralysis, and he sprinted back toward his office.

] [

The emus took all the blame. They were back in their paddock at dawn, but the tear in the fence made it clear they could've gotten out if they'd wanted to. And the testimony of the two survivors made it clear they had wanted to.

Leather Jacket and Long Hair also claimed to have been attacked by all kinds of birds. Long Hair said it was a hawk that had blinded his right eye. The coroner and police dismissed that part of their account. Most birds weren't active during the night. It was an owl that had half-blinded Long Hair, a Fish and Wildlife official pronounced, and the smaller scratches and lacerations were either glancing blows from the owl and emus or inflicted by the branches the men had blundered through on their way out.

Neither of the men who'd lived mentioned anything about a bird-human hybrid creature.

] [

Edmund stared at the box on the front stoop. He knew what was in it—he'd ordered it, after all.

But should I put it up?

Richard had been by the day before. Eyes on the ground, he'd mumbled an apology. He'd even offered to replace Edmund's bird feeder. Edmund had waved him off. He knew now what had really made the prints around his feeder, what had wrecked it trying to get to the seeds inside.

Warring impulses chased each other around Edmund's mind.

It did what you asked, so you should give it something in return.

But there's a man dead!

A man who desecrated the graves of veterans and cancer victims.

There's a new grave out there now, and it needs protection just as much as all the others.

In the end, what decided him was the memory of his grandmother. She talked about how her parents had always left a little bit of milk outside their front door, an offering for the People of the Mounds. *Things could go wrong if you didn't do that*, she'd said.

So, Edmund opened the box and took out the new bird feeder. It was a simple platform with a raised ridge around the edges to keep the seed from spilling off. It wasn't the least bit squirrel-proof, but Edmund suspected the squirrels would leave it alone—if they knew what was good for them. He set up the feeder and poured seed into it, a good mix of sunflower, millet, safflower, and cracked corn.

Then, he went to take down Barb's trail cam.

the last carnival

CALEB STEPHENS

The ocean is lustrous tonight—an endless mirror of dappled moonlight. The smell of salt fills your nose, along with brine and rust and the fresh night air.

They are good smells. Kind smells, unlike the place you wandered from. The place where they shuttle you between naps and meals and an endless assembly line of medications. To the people there, you are but a shadow—the faded afterimage of a life already spent.

Not here, though. *Here* you mean something.

Or you did. To someone. Once.

You turn from the pier and stare at the ancient skeleton of a rollercoaster. One with curves that used to glow in candy-apple reds and golds that flickered like the core of the sun. How you know this eludes you, so you retrieve the photo album you carry everywhere and flip through the pages until you are staring at a picture of this very shape. These very twists and bends. And you know by the way they sparkle and shine, you were right. It *was* alive—like you were so long ago.

Like you can be again. For a price.

You exhale and wipe the sweat from your hands, then focus your attention on the photo, willing it to take you with every wasted synapse your brain has left.

Every cell.

Every halting breath.

The throbbing starts first, as it always does, in a low hum at the base of your skull. A dull ache that spreads through your brain like an oil slick, the pressure behind your eyes building, growing so intense, so agonizing, you want to, *need to*, look away, but you don't. You force your eyelids wider instead, enduring the pain until—with a snap—*you are there.*

Dropping lower.

Feeling the rattle of the car on the tracks and the wind rushing through your hair.

Hearing the laughter and screams.

One comes from your right, and you turn—and see *her.*

And remember.

Kate. Her name is *Kate.*

The car slows to a stop, and she pulls you to your feet, into a sea of spinning rides. Smells rise all around you— buttered popcorn and spun sugar mixed with the savory tang of freshly grilled meat. You are young, as is she, and you both move with the easy freedom of youth as she tugs you onto the boardwalk, away from the crowd. When you reach it, she raises the camera that hangs from her neck and aims it at the ride you were on. *The Sea Dragon.* The camera flashes and spits out a plastic square which she shakes and presses into your hand.

"Here," she says. "So you don't forget me."

You open your mouth to tell her *never,* but she stretches on her tiptoes and silences you with a kiss. Sparks flood your bloodstream. Her lips are warm on yours. Her hair tickles your neck. Your pulse crashes behind your ears. Fireworks paint the sky in an orchestra of color. You want nothing more than to live in this moment forever. To hold onto it—onto *her*—and to never let it go.

But you can't. Already you feel the pull—like gravity in reverse—tugging at you, ripping you higher, coating the world in flat, lifeless tones. A thought ripples through your mind. *I need more time.*

You snap back into your body.

Your heart pounds with an irregular beat.

It takes a minute before you blink down at the photo album in your hands, at the charcoal square on the page leaking smoke. Your eyes narrow. Anger floods your chest. Something crucial has been taken from you. Some*one*. Only you don't know *who*. Or *why*. All you know is that it's gone, like the others that surround it, withering in a graveyard of blistered plastic.

A fresh belt of grief rises within you, and you contemplate tossing the album off the pier into the waves. You would be better without it, you think. You would no longer have to hurt. And you would, if it weren't for the still, small voice whispering that the pictures it contains are all that's left of you in this cold and empty world.

Your eyes burn as you stare across the blacktop at a familiar shape. A Ferris wheel. One that used to carry you to its apex and hold you there, cradled high atop the buttery glow of the city lights. It calls to you, this shape, so you shuffle toward it despite your aching knees and creaking back. You want to sit for a moment, to take a rest, but you don't dare. The men in uniforms will be looking for you soon, and this is the last time your broken and wasted body will carry you to this place that means so much.

Why does it mean so much?

The question haunts you. You should know. It's why you are here.

The album knows, you think. It always knows.

You pause and flip through the pages, stopping when you reach a photo of two strangers sitting on the chair of a Ferris wheel. One is a woman you judge to be in her thirties.

Striking but not beautiful, with a starburst of freckles scattered across her cheeks. Next to her is a man—also in his thirties—who reminds you of yourself. But not the you from the mirror, the you with cloudy eyes who gazes back lost and confused, with the hardpan face weathered by the years, and the lips weighted at the corners, too heavy to smile. This you is vibrant. This you is *alive*.

Splinters of light river your vision.

Your heart stalls and skips a beat.

And you are there once more, seated next to her, the two of you coasting ever higher. Above you, so far above, the fireworks burst with magnificent dollops of color. Electric blues and greens that remind you of fresh-cut grass. Except you aren't looking at them. You are looking at her, *only* at her.

It's been days, weeks, months, *years*, since you've last seen her—a lifetime since you were called away to serve your country.

"I'm sorry," she says, taking your hands in hers.

Anguish wells within you as you stare at the gentle swell of her belly, and the ring glittering on her finger. One given to her by another man, with a diamond larger than the ring you brought with you tonight, carefully tucked away in your jacket pocket for this very moment.

"Why?" you ask, dumbly. *"Why?"*

"I waited for you. I waited for so long. They told me you died. I had to move on." Her hand rises, and she gently brushes her knuckles across your cheek. "You were always the one. I'm so sorry."

Hooks pierce your skin in time with her words, followed by the odd sensation of jerking higher, watching as the two of you become pinpricks, and then vanish altogether.

Tears sting your eyes.

The penny-bright taste of blood pools on your tongue.

The oxygen won't come, won't fill your lungs, no matter how deeply you inhale. You place your gnarled fingers over your chest, over your heart, and wonder why it's beating like this. You are alone, surrounded by nothing but open air and metal skeletons. There's no one here who wishes you harm.

Still, a sliver of grief lodges in your throat. An echo of something, of someone, that pulls you toward the nearby tables nestled beneath several dead strings of light. You can't shake the feeling that you've been here before, in this very spot. On this very night.

You sit and reverently set the photo album on the table, then peel through the pages, all of which have turned cancerous and black. There's nothing here for you anymore, no more treasures to find. You've used them all up. But then you see it—a slash of color, centered on the final page. A single picture that steals your breath.

A voice wells from within and pleads for you to avert your eyes. To look away. To save this last sliver of your mind. This final vestige of *you.*

But you don't. You can't.

You have to *remember . . .*

The throbbing builds. A storm swells and lashes against the internal landscape of your skull. Lightning arcs in your mind and you are pulled into the photo with such a rush of pain, you don't know how you'll ever bear it.

But you do. And you are there, staring at her through unclouded eyes as the bright chime of carnival games flood your ears.

"We can't do this anymore," she says.

"Why . . . ?"

"You know why. It's not fair. To either of them."

Her gaze shifts to your hands, which are clasped in hers, and your stomach drops. There is a ring on your finger, and on hers. She has a husband and you have a wife—a tender-hearted woman, kind in all things, with a passion for animals and the less-fortunate. It's what attracted you to her in the first place—her incredible goodness, her zest for life. And, although you love her—and you *do* love her—she does not set your heart on fire the way this woman does. She does not make you feel this *alive.* Which is why Kate's words slam into you like a fist.

"But it's only once a year," you plead.

"That's the problem. It hurts too much. It's not enough time."

"So, leave him."

"You know I can't. And you can't leave your wife."

You open your mouth to reply, to tell her she's wrong, but it hangs there, slack. She's not wrong. There are children to consider. You both have separate lives.

Her face wilts, and her eyes turn pink at the edges. She stands. "It has to stop."

"I'll never stop coming," you say, rising with her. "I won't."

"Then you'll come alone." And you can tell by the way her lips quiver that she means it. There's a finality to her words. She's leaving a piece of herself here with you.

You raise a hand to stop her. "Kate . . ."

But she's already turned, is slipping away through the crowd.

The scene blurs and you fight to hold onto it, to *live* it again. And again. This is the last time you'll see her, the last precious memory you've managed to tuck away inside your ravaged mind.

Don't go, you think as the world curls at the edges. *Please stay.*

But it won't and it doesn't, and you watch helplessly as it all smokes and chars away. And then it's gone, and you sit alone in the dark, surrounded by the ghosts of this place: the abandoned vendor huts and decrepit rides. The faceless, empty signs.

Tears leak from your chin and patter off something on the table—a photo album. Or the approximation of one, holding nothing but page after page of blackened squares. Why anyone would keep such a thing is beyond you. It's a thought quickly swallowed by a series of booms splashing overhead, bursting across the night sky.

Fireworks, you think. *They're called fireworks.*

You watch them for a moment and wipe your eyes.

"Oh, my God. You came."

You startle and turn to find a woman staring at you with a face as old as your own, a lifetime of wrinkles rising through a layer of carefully applied makeup, her hair a burnished white. She looks at you like she knows you. Like she's seen you a thousand times.

"I can't believe you came," she whispers. "It's been so long."

You squint and try to place her face, but nothing comes. "Do I know you?"

Her light blue eyes widen in surprise. "Don't you recognize me?"

"No," you say. "Should I?"

"It's me. Kate."

Kate. She says it like it should mean something to you, this single syllable, this common name. But it means nothing, and the way she is staring at you, with such expectant weight, makes you feel uncomfortable, leaves you anxious and unsettled. You stand and move to leave, but she reaches out and places her hand on your arm, and pulls you to a stop.

"Wait . . . don't go. I'm sorry I haven't come in so long. I wanted to, but life . . . it got in the way." Tears glimmer in her eyes. One curls down her cheek. "You don't know how much I've missed you. We have so much to talk about. Please, you can't leave."

"I have to," you mumble.

And it's true. You do. You don't belong here with this strange woman, who looks at you like she's trying to memorize every curve and angle of your face, this woman who you've never seen before in your life. So, with a gentle motion, you ease her hand from your arm, and shuffle alone into the empty night.

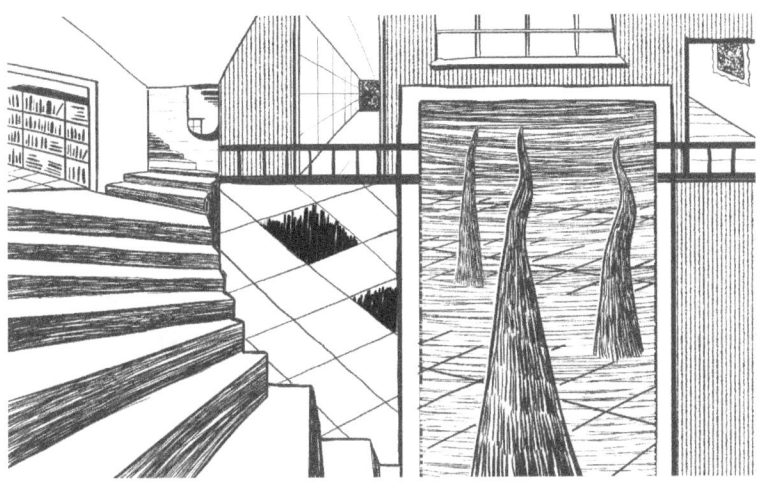

the Wings

RSL

RED

The pub is well into its Friday night reveries when I arrive. Smoke fills the halls, flutters out the windows, as everyone takes whatever intoxicants they can to forget the all-pervading red, green, and blue doors that took the world over twenty years ago, in 2004. People feel spectated—watched in rooms with blinded windows, in bathrooms where only tiles sit—and do everything they can to ignore that *l'appel du vide* that sings like sirens from the doors:

> open me, open me, they sing, *open me and join us in The Wings.*

If only they would listen.

Theo Cairns, retired Hallway Hunter, sits with a cigarette in her hand by one of the windows. She is alone, and she recognises me straight away, as if hungry for a friend. That will change soon enough.

"Gloves, on so hot a day?" she asks.

"I have a condition."

She laughs. "All you Wing nuts are the same," she tells me. "Got this look about you. Like you're still *in there*." She laughs. "You look familiar. You round here much?"

I tell her that I am everywhere, and admit I do bear a striking resemblance to a certain celebrity (trying my best to not reveal it was on a tragic BBC news headline). I then ask her the same question I will ask every participant in these shadowplay interviews. "Where were you when the Wings came?"

Theo nods, ready. "Shopping. In one of the big Tesco stores. Me Ma was, I don't know, gone. Down in the food aisles probably. I'd been at the magazines, reading, when one of the doors appeared . . ." Smoke drifts out of her mouth, unfurls toward the doorless hallways. "You know why they call it that, right?"

"Yes," I reply, more than she knows.

"The actor, Kaitlyn? We were friends once. I—I can't even remember what happened between us. I miss her—missed her." She looks outside. "She's a star now. Wasn't when I knew her, before she went inside. She came out different." She sips at her pint. "She used to be funny. She'd always impersonate me, you know? I liked that I could be impersonated, *read*. Like she was understanding me on some level."

She raises her hand. There is a burn on her finger. "We did this together, as kids. I dunno. It was stupid. A dare, that we both couldn't take a ciggie burn." She lights another on that Pavlovian impulse. "Became a bond, in a way. It was shit what happened to her—but still, I never liked the name she gave it. The Wings. As if here, now, is a stage. Hunters like me despise the name because we all know the truth. The doors, they all ooze that same light, don't they? That sickly red light, pooling, at the bottom of the door. Hunters, like us, we only ever call them one thing. *Escas*. Bait.

"So little eighteen year old me, looking for a distraction? Yeah, I saw the door and I did the most human thing in the world. I went in."

GREEN

"Where was I?" Dr. Davies, author of *Spatial Hostilities* and *The Metaphysics of the Wings* blinks, rubs his eyes, and looks up at me. "A seminar." He has been in and out of his chair since I came in, unnerved, as though the [green door] beside us might open of its own accord. "We all have stories of this nature, don't we? That brush with the unknown. Before the Wings, it was ghosts. Before ghosts, it was the fae. Before that, even, it was yellow eyes beyond the reach of the campfire.

"There's something *material* about it now though. All of us there, hapless and unaware as the the Wings appeared with their billions of RGB doors across the planet. There was no fear, really, no ominous implications to any of it, at the time that green door popped up in my office. Only, my curiosity nauseated me. Did you know that the Hunters call them Escas? The light of the anglerfish. *The lure.*

"There's nothing more alluring than a door, is there? *What's behind there, what's being kept from me . . .* So yes, it wasn't odd to see a door in a wall that day, where I was. Doors are manifold creatures that exist in a building for communication within itself. It was more the idea that it had literally manifested: that was laughable. I was a little green myself—not yet a tenured professor and instead a mere PhD student. I took to curiosity easier back then, like a child that hadn't been burned by fire yet. I only felt one thing: the drive we all feel, *to peer.*"

He clears his throat. Eyes turn foggy, that mind of his *elsewhere* now.

"Then I opened one."

A stranger might happen across the courtyard of the Knowsley Flatblock and think this place to be empty—a flatblock has, after all, a multiplicity of doors that the Wings rewire, distort, and replace. This building, however, is full. It is a council building—and so the careful removal of these new coloured doors is impossible. Removal is a luxury reserved only for government and corporate structures.

I am sat with Shaun Cullen in the courtyard. Across the way, a [blue door] smiles at us. Like many who have been forced to live at these low-income housing options, he has taken up the position of Runner, and this is why I am speaking with him.

"Running?" he responds. "It's basically a navigator. Hunters will go after displaced hallways in *our* world, but as a Runner, I live in there, mostly. Get a feel for it. Why'd you think the place is so clean, brother? I do bin runs in that place. Infinite tip disposal."

I nod, write as if I had been listening, and not imagining what it would be like to have him back in there, to have him with me. "Do you remember where you were, when the Wings arrived?"

"Too fucking right mate I know where I was. I was right here with a tinny. I'd just been sacked from me job, yeah, after I'd had a bit of a bad time an tha, and I came here, to me bird's. I was sat out here, though. I didn't wanna face her yet. And then just like tha, the door appeared in front of me, tha one, right there." The smiling [blue door] widens its grin.

"And you weren't scared?"

"Nah mate. Curious is all. I'm an Evertonian as well. Me family has always supported them—so, yeno, I'm partial to a blue door. Cut me and I *bleed* blue. Only felt natural to go open it."

RED

Theo lights another cigarette. "I'd never seen a room so red before. So quiet. I—I just thought it'd be a nice place to read, you get me? I went and grabbed my magazine, went back to the red room. I even closed the Esca behind me.

"The instant I did, though, everything *changed*. Like a shift in pressure when you come off an airplane somewhere abroad; the way the heat laps at your face, how gravity grabs at you a little more. Outside, the Esca was all charm. All handwaves and hugs. Inside? Doom. Panic attack levels of anxiety.

"It was the corners. They were too close, somehow. The room—I can barely remember it, even though I spent a whole day there, isn't that funny?—it was some sort of elongated hallway. Like someone took a small one and stretched it wide. Big *and* small. It was exactly like that dream you have before nodding off, where you shrink down and everything gets so big, but everything so big gets small, and you expand? Makes no sense—but that's the Wings for ye. And when the corners started to . . . *twist*, I couldn't breathe. I took stock of the room, to calm myself. I turned round to open up my door, that esca that lured me in.

"It was gone."

GREEN

"It wasn't so apocalyptic at the time," Dr. Davies says after another temperate silence. "It was all curiosity. I myself, as you know, was one of the first. Moseying on in like I hadn't a care in the world." His desk is reflected in his glasses, a smile on his lips starting to fade. "Mine was a library. An endless hexagonal structure that stretched up into a vault so high that even to look at it would fractalize your thoughts. To peer upward and to see that shape, endlessly repeating itself through each 'level' of the library . . . From the right angle, a spectator could see diagonally upward, to yet another column, and another . . ." He has been drawing on a sheet of paper for me. Hexagonal spiral-shapes circling up-and-outward. "And like that little librarian of Borges', I approached one of the walls. Took one of the books off the shelf."

"To find?"

The trees shiver outside in a gust of wind. Some class or other filters from a room. "Nothing," he says finally. "Nihil. In each and every book . . . nothing. The books, they split open directly in the middle of each; they were just toys. The faux library of Gatsby!" He sighs. "But I could have stayed in there for all eternity. Until the last star fizzled out. Could have stayed, to see if maybe one of those books *did* have something. Didn't Boltzman say that at the end of everything, there might be one moment of infinite regression? The second law of thermodynamics was always a little *sure* of itself. The ink in the water is always assumed to spread and make the whole cup cloudy, but there is a probability—even if it is one in a hundred, hundred billion—that the cloudy cup could once again return all that ink into one drop. Time does not exist, after all, in the subatomic world. What if this *library of nought* was but the preceding moments of *the library of everything*?"

BLUE

Shaun opens the [door]. Beyond, a massive gymnasium-sized space, and along the floor are sixteen evenly spaced three-by-three metre holes winking back. "See this?" Shaun picks up a wire leaking out of the [door]. "Theo—our mutual friend—she learned that lesson the hard way. Always keep a door wedged open." He invites me over. "Don't worry, we're perfectly safe," he assures me—despite my needing none in this homely place. He holds my hand as I step over the threshold. "Messes with the inner-ear," he says through a lit cigarette. "Always wondered if that was part of it, being *moved*." He squats by one of the holes, and tosses his cigarette into it. "Blacker than me nan's lungs, them."

"And this is one of the 'bin rooms'?" I ask.

"Oh aye," he replies. "As a Runner, this is probably one of the most useful rooms to me. That's why I wedged it open there. The doors have a habit of going missing when ye don't look at them. So the wedge keeps it there." His breath is very loud here. "You know, I heard something funny once. About these holes."

"Yeah?"

"Well—they're three-by-three metres, right?"

I nod.

He smiles. "That's the average size of a flatblock bedroom."

RED

"Sorry," says Theo, dazed. "I—I feel like I'm spacing out a lot." She eyes me up and down. Suspicious. "Where was I?"

"You had turned and found the door gone."

"Ah, yeah." Theo welcomes the two lagers I bought her and downs nearly half a pint in one go. "Those first few hours in the red. I'd been lost before, like. Loads of times. Went missing in Manny airport once, as a kid. But there were people there, ye get me? Someone you could tug on the sleeves of. Here? It was . . ." Theo slugs the rest of her beer. "I'd have stayed in that room. I really would have. Whenever I got lost that's all Ma said. *Don't fuckin move and we'll get you.* Well, see, there was this ringing in my ears. Back then, it scared the shit out of me. It came out of nowhere—and I knew straight away *this place* had given me it. I found another door after a while, and, I dunno, you should have felt what I felt. It was another door, but *not* the one I came in. It's counter-intuitive. If you use one door, you use that same door to get to where you were. But this other door, when I looked at it, the ringing in my ears went away, and at first I thought that was the way out. No ringing: no problem, yeah? But there was something else to it as well. In there, with everything being red, it was difficult to notice at first: but the door had that slight glow that had attracted me in the first place. My nerves were on edge, like I *needed* to stay there, to go toward *that* door, but..."

Theo stands, flushed, and leads me through the (doorless) pub entry. We stand outside as the air swirls crisp packets in eddies. From across the street, a waving red [door]. "You know what that ringing means," she says then. "It's a way back here. It's a call back *Home*. Back to the door you need.

"I still think about it sometimes. About . . . you know, what if I'd stayed? And worse, I think about . . ." Theo paused, finishing the rest of her lager in a rush before grabbing the second. Her knuckles were white, and her voice was low. "I think about what was trying to keep me there."

GREEN

"It's a good question," Dr. Davies replies. He shakes his head a little, as if he's just woken up. "I know I've tried to put that ringing in my ears behind me." He picks up his *Spatial Hostilities* book. "During my research, biologists and physicists all said the same thing. Inner-ear balance, the little bones, otoliths—it manipulates the inner-ear-fluid and, through that, electronic signals of movement, general balance, are generated. It's such a precise system, almost with the logic of computer science, and it was developed completely without funding and some project manager. Life did that—blind, random life. And, crossing over to this place, there's no greater indicator we *do not belong* when that ringing is there. Whether or not our balance knocked askew from fourth-dimensional transitioning (imagine moving a two-dimensional creature through the third dimension, eh?), or it's a version of yourself in decoherence, your possibilities now uncollapsed, et cetera, I do not know."

I am glad for the good doctor's rambles: at his desk, a newspaper has a face on the front. The face I'm wearing right now. "So what's your idea?" I ask, trying to keep him away.

"The way we think and access information has always been *feeling* first," he says, standing, moving apace. "We feel our way through to the knowledge we keep. We smell a perfume and think of an old flame, see a setting sun and think of all the suns that have set before . . . The answer, for me, is simple. Deprive the brain of any sort of stimulus, and it will begin to create where there is none. We will begin to *feel* that which is not there. Voices, whispers—ominous beasts lurking in the Wings . . ."

"So you don't believe that there are creatures inhabiting the Wings, doctor? Ghosts? The very 'spectators' that Kaitlyn Noone talks about in her book?"

"Of course not," he says. "The greatest danger of the Wings is ourselves." He closes his book. "The only ghosts in these empty spaces, I'm afraid, are us."

BLUE

Shaun sits on the edge of a hole. A little dizzy, he leans back. "Sorry—Can't even quite remember what you said." He looks around, sighs. "I didn't tell you the whole truth. You know that actor, Kaitlyn? The one who went missing? She was me bird. This—I feel strongly about this, I suppose. Seeing her like that. Got me down.

"She was bubbly. Weird in all the best ways. She did a boss impersonation of me, and Dr. Davies, too, actually. She had this character. *Sombre Umbridge*. She liked it. But when she finally escaped, when she started talking about the Wings as if there was something in there, watching us . . ."

"The spectators?" I ask, already familiar with you all.

He nods. "She spent *decades* in there. Alone. People can't be alone. They just can't. There's no lifeform in the universe that exists alone." Shaun's eyes are getting wet. I resist an urge to hug him. "Even solitary animals. They're just built up of cells. Always mutating. Atoms, ain't they—atoms looking at themselves. I always reckon the first cell that ever existed multiplied just to have someone to hold."

The door flaps against the line behind us; Shaun doesn't bother to look. His feet edge closer to the hole in front of us. "I miss her." He wipes his eyes. "Did you ever read her book?"

"I did."

"Mad, isn't it? It felt like someone else wrote it. Not the woman I knew. No wonder they found her with an arm and a leg gone. She was different. Not herself. Suppose that happens when ye lose your mind. Half way through, there was just, like, a hundred empty pages. I remember someone asked her about it, as if it was some literary thing, and she just said 'aren't pauses always that long?'

"It's like that saying. You are the closest people you know. And if she spent fifty years alone . . . I dunno. Sometimes I wonder, like—did she leave herself behind?"

I say nothing. He won't have much longer to wait.

"Or maybe . . . did something else get out?"

RED

Theo has returned to her seat.

"How long—in total—were you inside?" I ask.

Her head wavers left to right. "I—I never really knew. It felt like days of me running toward the ringing. Nowhere near as long as Kaitlyn though. I got into my head that wherever it was quiet, those Escas were *after* me. That the ringing was the only bit of safety.

"Every room, I avoided that glow. I passed through shopping centres, school hallways, fast food places. Some were unrecognisable twists of walls, stairs that led nowhere and bent in on themselves, ceilings that turned into floors. It was the idea of a room from someone who had never had to *be* in one. All of it red, all of it *distorted*. I was even in a car park at one point, except instead of spaces, it had great conical spires that slightly wiggled in some unfelt wind, stretching into the foggy blackness. Through it all, I followed the ringing, crying, getting proper emotional, and, just as I thought I was losing my mind, I burst out of these doors and returned to the magazines like it all had been a big fucking joke. I screamed bloody murder. Me Ma arrived after security called out me location. She arrived in a panic and I tells her. I just went missing, I nearly got caught. And even that surprised me—got caught by *what*?

"Someone else was approaching the door I'd just stumbled out of, and I just screamed at them *no, no, no*. Ma gave me a slap round the ear, she claimed I hadn't even been gone at all, that I was doing it for attention. It was only later I discovered I'd only been gone for ten minutes."

The scraping of glass against the bar's surface; bar staff fill pints; a teasing sensation of laughter (from faces we will never see) down by the pool table.

"So why did you become a Hallway Hunter?" I ask. "Is that not hard for you?"

Theo shrugs. "It's good money. When doors started going missing in big corporate buildings, when their hallways were being dislocated across the world—none of the white collars were gonna do it, were they? A rich white fella, what kind of panic has he had to endure? Me? Black, and from Liverpool—you grow up getting looked at. Getting stared at and talked about. You grow up always looking over your shoulder for wandering hands. Life in the Wings isn't much different. You just *know* there's someone watching. Some*ones* even. Like, you look up, and the ceiling doesn't feel like a ceiling—feels like you're in the middle of this box that is transparent from both sides and there is this . . . this feeling that you're looking up at *them,* Kaitlyn's *spectators.* it's like looking up at the night sky."

I smile, for she is so close. "Like seeing a cosmos of eyes?"

GREEN

"How is she?" asks Dr. Davies, after (what he must assume has been) a long silence. "Sorry, it's just—I felt I needed to ask that."

"Theo, you mean?"

"Yes, yes."

A brief pause. "She returned to the Wings, doctor."

Dr. Davies' polite composure falls away—a frown sullies his face. "That undiscovered country," he says—but oh how little he knows of the Wings, of death, even now. I wish I could help elucidate on its nature. I will, in time. "She was a good student. Still is," Dr. Davies adds. "She can always return. We all can." He stands and looks outside. The sky is very grey. "You know, you look so familiar. What's your name?"

"Umbridge," I say.

"Umbridge." He laughs. "You're not a detective in a novel, are you?"

Shaun tosses another cigarette down into the hole. Out goes that brief little light. "How is he, anyway, me old tutor?"

"He began research for a new book." I clear my throat. "He went in search of the library."

"Shit. I—I hadn't heard." Shaun flicks another cigarette down the hole. "He was always obsessed. Thought that he'd find some, like, 'totality,' he always said. At the beginning, you couldn't get him out of there. That's where I got the idea to be a Runner—there's some weird time dilation shit that happens, and so students have a lot of time to cram in research before an exam in there. May as well get some use out of Kaitlyn being gone for fifty years, even though she was only actually missing for five days." The hole stretches like an unfolding scab before us. "I hope he gets out. There's still a chance, you know? Kinda reminds me about that other theory of his. The one about, erm, realising . . ."

RED

"Oh, that's shit," says Theo, when I tell her the bad news. "Shaun was a good mate." She's swinging a little side to side now. "What was it?"

"They think he lost his door," I say. "That he's still Running through to find a way out."

She nods, grave. "We had the same tutor. Did Shaun tell you that? Dr. Davies. Saw he went the same way, not long ago. Funny." She's watching me now.

The moves I make. The pencil marks I scribble.

Her brow creases in sudden suspicion. "What is this for again?"

GREEN

"It's just that I had been playing with this theory, for my new book." Dr. Davies still is staring at the sky, that long, slender granite slab reaching over the horizon like a ceiling. Red and green and blue [doors] pop out against the urban greyscape below. "This place, it used to be packed. Alive. Emptiness fills it up."

"Are you referring to the decreasing population, Doctor?"

"Decreasing?" he laughs. "There are more disappearances now than there are births. And if people *do* come back, they come back like Kaitlyn. Sans limbs—and a long wait of relearning how to speak." He takes a moment. "See out there, how bereft those streets are of people? No one is stupid enough to even go within five metres of one of those doors. They're not idly wandering in there like children. No. I think something is reaching out. Something is pulling them in.

"Something is feeding."

BLUE

"I have heard that theory," I reply to Shaun. "What are your thoughts on it?"

"That the Wings can *leak out*? I know Davies worked on another one, to do with the RGB colour model. Simulation shit." He drags on another cigarette. "I started seeing the stars at night as little holes in a box."

At the edge of the room, the ceiling and the walls twist all together in a single line.

"You know how dark matter and dark energy takes up, like, 95% of the universe's material? What if this is it? What if there's just, I don't know, endless halls, between the grand stages of life?" He smiles, like he's made a joke. "Reminds me. Dr. Davies loved this theorist, Mark Fisher. Fisher read to us at a lecture once. This was some time after they had removed all the doors, when the hallways were going missing. And Fisher, he comes in and shakes Davies' hand. Turns to the class and he says, 'we've lost all exits.' We laughed at it then. Had to. Cry or laugh, they say.

"He was right, I reckon. That's why I feel safer in here, than out there. Even that *Wing dread* or whatever. It's just—it's normal. I've got nothing out there. I'm just alone. Alone without Kaitlyn.

"I'm already lost."

RED

"It's research on how the Wings have shaped society," I tell Theo. "Accounts like yours are very important. Which is why I must ask of you one thing."

"Like?"

"Would you show me your work one last time?"

"No," Theo says, "In fact—"

GREEN

His hand starts to rub where a wedding band sits. "Did you ever see that first interview with Kaitlyn Noone? After she had been missing for three days or so. I remember watching those side-by-sides of Kaityln as this twenty-something TikTokker, then as she was at seventy years old mere days later. I—I couldn't help but laugh at the ridiculousness of the whole thing. It was just so dramatic. So unreal. She had lost an arm and a leg—literally—with no real signs of trauma to the skin. There's no cut, no scar. For all intents and purposes, the arm and leg simply forgot to be there."

I tap my leg and fingers to a rhythm; I nod.

"That first interview with her—people have said she seems to be *lesser*. Scatter-brained. Like she had lost something in her mind, some neuronal pathway. The way she spoke. She was so fluent and almost regal-sounding at first. Now? Words seemed new to her. When she spoke, she spoke like she was sounding them out with a new tongue.

"The holes inside a slice of cheese, the gap inside a bell: these are seemingly empty spaces that are *real*. What if Katilyn had *acclimatised* to these spaces; is this not what happens when we are surrounded by objects? When, like Baudrillard would come to say, we become but a system of relations between objects? Can we become a system of relations between *absences*? If a space conditions us, what does emptiness do? Do we swallow it, become (w)hole? You've seen those returns. The people after Kaitlyn. They need *refilling*, almost.

"Kaitlyn said something in that interview. '*It passed like the sleep of a closed door yet to open.*' She said she couldn't remember her life. That she didn't even know that boy, Shaun, her boyfriend. She didn't know how to eat, drink, or expel 'used products' so to speak. But when she did learn. When she began to speak and those motor functions returned . . . That interview is enlightening. Can a door *sleep*? If space conditions people, then don't people condition space?

"What if a door could *think*, could *love*? What if the four walls of a room could learn it is so empty inside, and wants only to be full? To be whole?"

"I'm afraid I'm not quite visualising it, Doctor. Could you perhaps use that door in the corner of your office?"

Dr Davies smiles, warily. "I'm—I'm not too partial to the door these days. I've lost a lot of good students there. Some of the best." He looks down at a paper. Then looks back up at me. Finally, he sees it. Sees me. "I . . . I don't understand," he says.

"I think you do."

BLUE

"So where is the door now?" I ask Shaun. "Because the line wedging it open is gone."

"Wait, what?" His eyes flare up. "Why—why is it gone?"

RED

"Show me how you do your work, Theo."

She looks side to side, like she's walking out of a fog. "I—we were at the bar."

"And now we are in the Wings."

"How—"

"You had a drink and I asked you to show me your work. You said you knew 'just the place.'"

"Did I? I—" she nurses her head. "The ringing is so bad right now."

"Look at me," I say, taking off my right glove.

And Theo sees the burn on my finger, the same as hers.

GREEN

"I'm glad you took us into the Wings, Doctor, to further illustrate your point."

The old man gawps upward. Only a great billowing night looks back, presses down as if it were the surface of some planet always and forever falling. Besieging him from all sides are many millions of houses, long great aisles of them. So many [doors], so many little spaces to crawl through. The one to his office is so far away. If it was ever there at all.

"Why are we here?" he asks. "I—I don't do this. Can't do this. Get me out."

"You led *me* here, Doctor. There is something you are trying to tell me."

"No—just—just who are you anyway?"

"An old friend."

BLUE

"Did you kick the line?" he screams.

"Shaun," I say, "you don't have to be sad anymore." And I smile using half of Kaitlyn's face.

RED

"How—that's, that's, that's Kaitlyn's arm. How do you—Are you Kaitlyn?"

I laugh as my shadow grows. "Not *just* her."

GREEN

"I'm just using its face," I say. "But I'm some of what you miss. And other things too. I'm some of your best students."

His eyes light up when I begin to shine.

"Was that *you?*" Shaun shouts. "Did—" he throws up. "I feel so—so *unhere*, like I'm being falling asleep. What the *fuck* is—"

RED

"The face, from the news," she bellows through a form that is slowly falling away. "Get away from me! You took her; you *took* her."

"Don't be angry," I reply, a hand on hers as we melt into the glorious vacuity of the Wings. "I'm what she left behind."

GREEN

Dr. Davies stares at the books in their endless numbers—that smile like an addict's relapse. A tremor at his lips: he's scared.

"It's okay," I say. "We're here, Doctor, all of us. And we can find the library of everything together."

BLUE

"It can't be," screams Shaun, weeping. "It's not you. It can't be. I lost you. I *lost* you."

But we haven't gone anywhere. "And you found me again," I say, our hands knotting like playdough.

REDGREENBLUE

The bar where Theo Cairns sat is empty. The few who took notice of her, in their abyssal plunge into little intoxicants, move on and away.

A vigil is held at the University of Liverpool for one Dr. Davies. What a good man, they say. A good man lost to the peril of the Wings. He died for his research.

And there is the empty yard of the flatblock. Shaun-less, filled with litter and rot and bits of skull. With no runner, the occupants are trapped in rooms displaced by the Wings. It is easier to jump through the window, than to go wandering in the Wings alone. But soon, I will help them see.

I remember when I struggled with the gift given to me. This great space that they all think so empty.

Some of us clamour and shout:
what used to be [Shaun] blurring with [Kaitlyn],
[Dr. Davies] devolving back into [Theo]—
A million voices lost in the Wings, smudging into one
colour:
we are the red-hot anger for a world given up;
we are the green naïveté of minds too curious to care;
and we are the blue melancholy of lovers lost to the
suddenness of empty space.
we are long hallways on silent Tuesday nights,
empty bars on hungover Sunday mornings,
and abandoned housing lots where
the lonely saunter in left-alone Friday nights.

Don't be afraid should a [door] open and you are there, by
yourself.
You are only one whine of a hinge away from never being
alone again.

editor's note

Perhaps appropriately, for a long while this anthology floated in a developmental purgatory, neither here nor there. It was my first attempt at editing together a community project solo—as compared to *Collage Macabre: an Exhibition of Art Horror*, which was a true collaborative effort. Many talented folks all working at the top of their game pitched in to realize that book, including myself, but much of the practicalities of publication were taken up by impressively-skilled project managers. I handled the aspects of that process I enjoyed— the sequencing of titles, liaising between artists and authors on illustrations for stories, creating graphic design for promotion and marketing—but this project was different. It taught me more than I can articulate about myself and my own workflow, not to mention where my boundaries are and how wildly my bandwidth can vary from day to day.

This book started with over twenty writers, each eagerly anticipating a chance to try their hand at the theme. (The zeitgeist is all over so-called "liminal spaces," with frequent visuals of the Backrooms and abandoned properties insinuating their way into everyone's social media feed.) Somewhere along the way, however, various issues cropped up and we lost a few authors to the *hallways*. Yet, despite that loss, we persisted, and we would not be here without the help of many kind folks who served as clarion calls through the dim.

First, and foremost, my eternal gratitude to PL McMillan, esteemed proprietor of Salt Heart Press, who threw me a rope when I felt immured in quicksand; also to Molly Halstead, whose formatting and typesetting skills continue to be indispensable in my publishing journeys. To Chelsea Pumpkins and Alexis DuBon, whose friendship and advice in editorial matters—and otherwise—continues to be an unwavering light. To D. Shaw, whose name is Legion (for they are many), continuing to remind that community is paramount in most creative endeavor.

To the magnificent artists on display here: to Mary Sanche, for her incredible work on the cover art—to say that it exceeds my wildest expectations is an understatement. To schism, whom I continue to return to, and for good reason: her interpretations of the written word via interior illustration are always sensitive, thoughtful, and awe-inspiring. There is no mechanical replacement—and there never will be—for the human ability when it comes to art, and I am blessed to be able to work with such talented, professional artists.

Lastly—and I think I speak for not only myself here, but all of those involved in this creative endeavor—to our supportive partners, family, friends, beloved animal companions. Without them, our compulsion to explore these haunted places might lead us to endless wandering.

Instead, their beacons bring us home.

about the authors

MOB writes, codes, and boulders. Work found on The Dread Machine, Pseudopod, and Translunar Travelers Lounge. Very occasionally on Twitter @mob_writes.

DEMI-LOUISE BLACKBURN is a dark fiction author from a small, tired town in West Yorkshire, England. Outside of writing, you'll find her skulking online, collecting questionable and potentially haunted knick-knacks for her office, which is lovingly dubbed 'The Smile Room'. Find her at demi-louise.com.

CARSON WINTER is an award-winning author, punker, and raw nerve. His short fiction has appeared in over 20 publications, including *Apex*, *Vastarien*, and *Chthonic Matter Quarterly*. He is the author of *Soft Targets, The Psychographist*, and *A Spectre is Haunting Greentree*.

ELOU CARROLL is a graphic designer and freelance photographer who writes. Her work appears or is forthcoming in *The Deadlands, Baffling Magazine, In Somnio: A Collection of Modern Gothic Horror* (Tenebrous Press), *Ghostlore* (Alternative Stories Podcast) and others. When she's not whispering with ghosts, she can be found editing *Crow & Cross Keys*, where she publishes all things dark and lovely, and spending far too much time on Twitter (@keychild). She keeps a catalogue of her weird little wordcreatures on www.eloucarroll.com.

REBECCA CUTHBERT writes dark fiction and poetry. Her books include *In Memory of Exoskeletons, Creep This Way: How to Become a Horror Writer with 24 Tips to Get You Ghouling*, and *Self-Made Monsters*. For publications, reviews, events and more, visit rebeccacuthbert.com.

IVY GRIMES is from Georgia, and her collection *Glass Stories* is available from Grimscribe Press. Feel free to visit her at www.ivyivyivyivy.com.

JULIE SEVENS is a horror writer and an everything reader. The tentacular appendages of the universe have moved her from Ohio to Philadelphia to Berlin. Now just beyond the interstellar blast-zone of Chicago, Julie lives with her husband, two sons, a doorstep spider named Lentil, and a ghost in the closet who resists naming. She sews and does embroidery, and has always been more of a crafter than an artist. Find more of her nightmares at julie-sevens.com.

ALEX WOLFGANG is a horror author from Oklahoma City. His debut collection, *Splinter and Other Stories*, is available now. You can find his work in *Cosmic Horror Monthly* and *Nocturnal Transmissions Podcast,* as well as in the anthologies *Howls from Hell, Bloodlines, Fiends in the Furrows III: Final Harvest,* and *Collage Macabre.* When not reading and writing horror, you can find him hiking and camping, playing tennis, and watching movies with his wife. You can follow him on Twitter @ alexwolfgang, on Instagram @alex__Wolfgang, or visit his website at www.alex-wolfgang.com.

S.E. DENTON is a UX/UI designer by day and a horror writer by night. She lives in Tulsa with her two cats. She can be found on Twitter @infinitedent.

ANGELA SYLVAINE is a self-proclaimed cheerful goth who writes speculative fiction and poetry. Her debut novel, *Frost Bite*, and her debut short story collection, *The Dead Spot: Stories of Lost Girls* are available now. Her short fiction and poetry have appeared in or on over fifty anthologies, magazines, and podcasts, including *Southwest Review, Apex,* and *The NoSleep Podcast.* You can find her online at angelasylvaine.com.

JOSEPH ANDRE THOMAS is a writer and literature professor living in Vancouver, British Columbia. He is a graduate of the University of Toronto's MA in Creative Writing program. A recipient of the Avie Bennett Emerging Writer scholarship and the Canada Master's scholarship, Joseph's writing has appeared in the anthologies *Howls from Hell, Howls from the Wreckage, Howls from the Scene of the Crime, Collage Macabre, Black Cat,* and *The Darkness Beyond the Stars.*

KEN HUELER teaches kung fu in the San Francisco Bay Area, where he also co-chairs the local Horror Writers Association chapter. His work has appeared in *Weirdbook, The Sirens Call, Space & Time, Weekly Mystery Magazine, Andromeda Spaceways,* and anthologies such as *The Cozy Cosmic* and *Tales for the Camp Fire*. With Frances Lu Pai Ippolito, he is co-editor of the game fiction anthology *Winding Paths: A Playable Reading Experience*. You can learn more at kenhueler.wordpress. com.

ERIK MCHATTON's passion for horror literature began in grade school and can be credited to an early fascination with the "Terrific Triples" horror collections of Helen Hoke. He began writing fiction seriously in 2019 and has since been published several times in print and online publications. He hopes to follow in the footsteps of authors like Ligotti, CAS, Bloch, Jackson, Barker, and Cushing. He lives in Kentucky with his beautiful wife and kids, along with dear friends and family; surrounded on all sides.

CHRISTI NOGLE is the author of the Shirley Jackson Award-nominated and Bram Stoker Award®-winning First Novel *Beulah* from Cemetery Gates Media and the collections *The Best of Our Past, the Worst of Our Future; Promise;* and *One Eye Opened in That Other Place,* from Flame Tree Press. She is co-editor (with Willow Dawn Becker) of the Bram Stoker Award®-nominated anthology *Mother: Tales of Love and Terror,* and co-editor (with Ai Jiang) of *Wilted Pages: An Anthology of Dark Academia.* Follow her at https://christinogle.com and on social media @christinogle.

NINA SHEPARDSON is an Active Member of the SFWA. Her short fiction appears or is forthcoming in *Vastarien, Cosmic Horror Monthly,* and the BSFA's *Fission* anthology series, among others. She blogs at ninashepardson.substack.com. Nina lives in New England with her husband.

CALEB STEPHENS is an award-winning author writing from Denver, Colorado. His novels include *The Girls in the Cabin*, a psychological thriller available through Joffe Books, *Feeders*, a speculative horror thriller available through Timber Ghost Press, and *If You Lie*, a thriller from Thrillerscape Press. His fiction collection *If Only a Heart and Other Tales of Terror* is available through Salt Heart Press and includes the short story "The Wallpaper Man," which was adapted to film by Falconer Film & Media in 2022. His next novel, *Soul Couriers*, is forthcoming from Dark Matter INK in 2025. You can join his mailing list and learn more at calebstephensauthor.com, as well as follow him on Instagram @calebstephensauthor.

RSL is a writer and academic of weird, absurd fiction. When he isn't avoiding his PhD work, he's writing about his nightmares and playing games. He is also an associate editor with *Haven Spec Magazine*. You can find him at @rsljnr on Twitter and bluesky, or in his work published—or forthcoming—in *Cosmic Horror Monthly, Vastarien, Nightmare Magazine,* and *Apparition Lit.*

reading advisories

MOB — PLAY SPACE
allusions to abuse

DEMI-LOUISE BLACKBURN — FUN-A-LOT
allusions to abuse/sexual abuse, gore

CARSON WINTER — THE DEATH FACTORY
none

ELOU CARROLL — - .... . / - .... .. -. --. / .-- .. - .... / . -.-. ....
--- . ...
none

REBECCA CUTHBERT — THE HOLE HAD ALWAYS BEEN THERE
grief, death of a parent

IVY GRIMES — GLASS DOOR
grief, death

JULIE SEVENS — QUEUE
none

ALEX WOLFGANG — OUT OF CONTEXT
none

SE DENTON — PORTAL
alcoholism, drug use

ANGELA SYLVAINE — #BLESSED
confinement

JOSEPH ANDRE THOMAS — THE LIGHTS
none

KEN HUELER — "DEMON!" IT SHRIEKED
blood, abduction, murder

ERIK MCHATTON — WHERE WE WERE, WHERE WE ARE, WHERE WE WILL ALWAYS BE
blood, bullying, cancer, child abuse, abortion, death

CHRISTI NOGLE — THE HALLS
none

NINA SHEPARDSON — THE BARROW-KEEPER
none

CALEB STEPHENS — THE LAST CARNIVAL
none

RSL — THE WINGS
addiction, grief, manipulation

further reading

MOB —

"The Red Lady" — *Collage Macabre: An Exhibition of Art Horror*

"Free Party, Late" — *Cosmic Horror Monthly*

DEMI-LOUISE BLACKBURN —

"The Rotten Cradle" — *Welcome to Your Body: Lessons in Evisceration*

"Josie" — *Collage Macabre: An Exhibition of Art Horror*

CARSON WINTER —

The Psychographist

Soft Targets

A Spectre is Haunting Greentree

Posthaste Manor (with Jolie Toomajan)

"The Guts of Myth" (Split Scream vol. 1)

ELOU CARROLL —

"You Hope, Through Shivers and Sweat" — *Haven Spec Magazine*

"Clack Clack Clack" — *Maudlin House*

REBECCA CUTHBERT —

In Memory of Exoskeletons

Self-Made Monsters

IVY GRIMES —

Glass Stories

Star Shapes

"Rags to Riches" — *Odd Jobs: Six Files from the Dept. of Inhuman Resources*

JULIE SEVENS —

"Lady Widow" — *Collage Macabre: An Exhibition of Art Horror*

"Early Adopter" — *Welcome to Your Body: Lessons in Evisceration*

"Falling" — *34 Orchard*

ALEX WOLFGANG —

"Chiaro Obscuro" — *Collage Macabre: An Exhibition of Art Horror*

"The Hollow March of Decay" — *Welcome to Your Body: Lessons in Evisceration*

"The Heads of Leviathan" — *Bloodlines: Four Tales of Familial Fear*

Splinter and Other Stories

The Neighbors (as Alex Witcher)

S.E. DENTON —

"Madame Crystal" — *AHH! That's What I Call Horror: an Anthology of 90s Horror*

ANGELA SYLVAINE —

The Dead Spot: Stories of Lost Girls

Chopping Spree

Frost Bite

JOSEPH ANDRE THOMAS —

"The Preparator" — *Collage Macabre: An Exhibition of Art Horror*

"Locked Out" — *The Darkness Beyond the Stars*

"Casualties of a Predictable Apocalypse" — *Howls from the Wreckage*

"Motive Factor X" — *Howls from the Scene of the Crime*

KEN HUELER —

"Infinity of Worse" — *The Lost Librarian's Grave*

ERIK MCHATTON —

"These Little Tyrants" — *Odd Jobs: Six Files from the Dept. of Inhuman Resources*

"Station 42" — *Collage Macabre: An Exhibition of Art Horror*

"Straw World" — *Vastarien*

"The Man Who Collected Ligotti" — *Cosmic Horror Monthly*

CHRISTI NOGLE —

Beulah

The Best of our Past, the Worst of Our Future

Promise

One Eye Opened in That Other Place

NINA SHEPARDSON —

"Paint It Red" — *Collage Macabre: An Exhibition of Art Horror*

"Stoneborn" — *Vastarien*

"Music of the Spheres" — *Cosmic Horror Monthly*

CALEB STEPHENS —

If Only a Heart and Other Tales of Terror

Feeders

The Girls in the Cabin

If You Lie

"Future Portraits of the Unhappy Dead" — *Odd Jobs: Six Files from the Dept. of Inhuman Resources*

RSL —

"Der Zedernwald" — *Cosmic Horror Monthly*

"He Will Not Fall Until . . ." — *Cosmic Horror Monthly*

"Darnsworth Products" — *Apparition Lit Magazine*

"Consummation" — *Howls from the Scene of the Crime*

"We Factories of Pain" — *Nightmare Magazine*

about the editor

TJ PRICE's corporeal being is currently located in Raleigh, NC, where he lives with his handsome partner of many years, but his ghosts can be found in northeastern Connecticut, southern Maine, north Brooklyn, and the corner of your eye. He is the author of *The Disappearance of Tom Nero*, a novelette, and has work published in venues such as *Nightmare Magazine*, *PseudoPod, Cosmic Horror Monthly,* and various anthologies and assorted grimoires. In addition, he has served as editor on a number of projects, including the anthologies *Collage Macabre: an Exhibition of Art Horror* and *Odd Jobs: Six Files from the Department of*

Inhuman Resources. He is currently working on editing Emma E. Murray's forthcoming début collection *The Drowning Machine and Other Obsessions,* as well as Erik McHatton's forthcoming début collection *Straw World and Other Echoes from the Void,* both to be published with Undertaker Books. He also serves as Assistant Editor at *Haven Speculative Magazine.* Future projects include whispering of the red tower, a book of poetry, and a possible collection of his own screb fiction. One may invoke him at either tjpricewrites.com, or go to the darkest place you know and whisper his name—please note, he cannot be held responsible for what may answer.

Salt Heart Press

"Invention, it must be humbly admitted, does not consist in creating out of void but out of chaos."

— *Mary Shelley*

We at Salt Heart Press seek the best in horror. We live for it, we crave it, we desire it — nothing gives us more pleasure than the thrills and chills found in the perfectly crafted dark tale. As such, it is our mission to seek out fresh voices in the genre, search out the new and unique, the brave and challenging. We want to be scared. We want to be haunted. And we want the same for you.

So take a look at the books we have and keep an eye out for those to come.

https://www.saltheartpress.com/

Check out these other spooky books from Salt Heart Press

What Remains When The Stars Burn Out
a horror collection by P.L. McMillan

If Only a Heart and other tales of terror
by Caleb Stephens

Confirmed Sightings: a triple cryptid creature feature
featuring Bridget D. Brave, P.L. McMillan, and Ryan Marie
Ketterer

**The Darkness Beyond The Stars: an anthology of space
horror**
edited by P.L. McMillan

Welcome To Your Body: Lessons in Evisceration
edited by Ryan Marie Ketterer